The Golden Horn

by
Michael Wescott Loder

PublishAmerica
Baltimore

ISBN: 1-4241-8927-6
PUBLISHED BY PUBLISHAMERICA, LLLP
www.publishamerica.com
Baltimore

Printed in the United States of America

Acknowledgments

A deep "thank you" for my wife, Linda, for her endless support, and for taking the picture of myself that appears on the back cover.

A special thanks also to my children, Laura, Lisa and Scott—long my first readers—and my son-in-law, Stephen Eastman, for his help in Photoshop with the cover art.

A thank you to my staff and faculty colleagues and friends at Penn State Schuylkill, supporters of my writing throughout the many years I have served this campus of the Pennsylvania State University. This especially includes Stephen Couch, for the loan of his french horn that appears in the cover art.

And a final thank you for my friends and fellow travelers in the Eastern PA chapter of the Society of Children's Book Writers and Illustrators for their never ending support and encouragement. I am not there yet, but the road has an end, and the journey is part of the reward.

Note:

The Turkish Invasion of Austria and Hungary in 1683 and Turkish actions in the Balkans in the late 17th Century were actual historical events. All other events, including the country of Starnovia, its history and its characters, are fiction.

Contents

Part I: Noviastad

Chapter 1

The Girl: The stranger was obviously a foreigner, for no one in my country could afford the jacket and denim trousers he wore under his loden green cloak. I watched him walk to the bar and speak to Madam Sophie before taking a seat in the second booth. He must be strong in courage but weak in wisdom to pick her, I told myself. His wallet was in his left rear pocket, and he was seated with that hip to the outside. He would be my victim tonight. I just wished he was not so young and nice-looking.

Madam Sophie started the softening up with a tall stein of our better beer, not too strong and unadulterated. Then she sat down across from him and began her usual questions and witty remarks. I moved right, setting my feet down carefully, my eyes never leaving the boy's face. Once I was behind him, I relaxed slightly, but kept the silence even when I reached the first booth with its darkened curtains. Sliding onto one of its padded benches, I started my wait.

Madam Marie joined Sophie. Together, the two soon had him laughing and started on a second steinful. I could hear the clatter of his coins as he fumbled and dropped them onto the table. He was some kind of scholar, a student at a university in America, I heard him tell them. He was staying at the Golden Horn Hotel but would be leaving soon.

The sound of the stein being refilled again told me that the moment for me to work my part had come. I took several deep breaths and rubbed my hands together, trying to dry away the sweat. If only …if only it worked this time. Last chance, Jonnie. You miss, you die. Please, let the drink have done its part. Please, Lord of thieves, guide my fingers now …

The Student: "Present company excepted, of course," I replied with another lift of my stein. I smiled at the closest of my new lady friends and she grinned back, showing several blackened teeth and a twist to her lips. What a place, what marvelous people! I smiled more broadly before bringing my left hand down sharply on the fingers trying to edge their way into my pants pocket.

The owner of the fingers squealed like a kicked pig and rolled away to sit up on the dirty floor where she crouched, nursing her hand and glaring at me. My companions ignored her. "Another drink, Master Scholar? Another?" they pleaded.

I opened the stein's lid and studied its contents then snapped the lid shut before the pitcher heading in my direction could quite reach the pouring stage. "No, thank you. I must resist." I got to my feet, bowed to the nearest woman—whose smile had taken on a tormented look—and headed for the portal labeled with a red exit light.

She tried once more, following me, grasping my arm and turning her body so that the view down the front of her dress went all the way to Jerusalem. I twisted and left her clinging to a wire-backed chair that she had to catch to avoid crashing to the floor. "So long, sweetheart. The pleasure was all mine," I called out and threaded my way through the swinging door.

I walked, steady now on my feet, wishing for a john but confident that I had enough time to make my hotel. Gad! I had been stupid! Stupid to think that I could have fun with these sweet-talking people less than three years after a destructive war had ruined even the richest families. I patted my sides where my dirk and passport holder hung to assure myself that I had lost nothing and increased the size of my steps. "You know-it-all-asshole," I mumbled to myself, and kicked a power pole as I passed by it.

A block from my hotel's back entrance I heard shoes slapping the pavement behind me. I paused, then stepped into an alcove formed by a once grand entrance to an office building. A slender shadow faded behind a pillar. I waited only a second, for I could see no point in staying put. The lights that marked my hotel's entrance promised safety. I headed toward them, picking up my pace as I did. The sounds behind me resumed and sped up.

Five feet from the nearest light, I pivoted against a wall and had my dirk drawn in one spinning movement. With a yip, my follower attempted a skidding stop, but flipped on her backside instead as I lodged a shoe between her ankles. I treated her shoulder like a soccer ball, and she went flying—her head smacking a granite wall with a thunk like a dropped melon.

After several deep breaths, I managed to steady myself enough to check the damage. My would-be assailant lay unmoving, her pencil-thin arms and legs flopped on the pavement like a puppet's limbs after its strings are cut, her face flattened against the sidewalk. I knew her too—she was the same skinny scum who had tried to get intimate with the contents of my pants pocket not ten minutes earlier. Well, she had been coming after me—not I after her—I reminded myself angrily. I resheathed my dirk and backed slowly toward the hotel entry.

Standing under the light of the white globes that marked civilization, I relaxed and again studied my would-be attacker. She appeared somewhere in age between thirteen and fourteen with long, dark, tangled hair but pale skin. She wore a loden green cloak similar to my own but smaller and of cheaper material. Underneath I could just make out her gray and yellow striped dress. Tire-treaded sandals completed an outfit not much different than those worn by almost all the women I had already seen in this sad, impoverished country. I sighed and was about to turn away when I noticed the blood starting to trickle out of her nose.

Chapter 2

I groaned, staring at the dark red puddle growing under her mouth. The sweat of my previous anger and fear now felt cold and wet against my back, its smell mixing with the street's odors of stale beer and blocked sewers. "Oh, crap," I whispered to myself. I glanced through the glass doors toward the lobby and the registration desk; I looked down and up the street. This girl and I were still alone.

Sucking in my breath, I eased back to where she lay. I checked my surroundings again before kneeling and gently shaking the nearest shoulder. She let out a moan.

"Are you all right?" I asked her softly in her own language.

Her head rolled to the left and a flinch of pain furrowed her forehead, but she did not open her eyes. Others were now in sight—still a block or more away—but walking toward me. What was I to say to them? I had the only weapon; she was the injured one. I had heard enough stories about the way Starnovian police and courts treated foreign nationals to know that this was not a place to be.

Sometimes we do things that we later can only describe as asinine or crazy. I scooped up the girl and, cradling her in my arms and against my chest, walked back to the hotel entrance and stepped inside. Without giving the registration clerk any chance to react, I turned a corner and started up the main stairs. Reaching the mezzanine, I hit the elevator button.

The elevator ran quickly. For that I was grateful, and my sense of relief increased when I stood inside my own room and heard the door's lock click home. For a few seconds I closed my eyes, aware of how heavy what I was carrying now felt.

When my heart had stopped pounding, I carried my guest through the entry hall and into my room. There I lowered her onto my double bed's feather-filled comforter. She was awake and returned my gaze with half-opened but still glazed eyes before rolling onto her back and spreading out her arms—like a child about to sweep a snow angel. She let out a whimper and closed her eyes once more.

Maybe she would stay there a while. I retreated to the bathroom. I used the head, then turning to the sink, pulled out my dirk and laid it on the counter—just in case. The native term for these nasty knives with their twelve inch blades was actually *Dirkosgay*. I had yet to see any male citizen without one. I had been provided with my own by my first host within hours of my arrival. Mine was typical of the type—slender-bladed, with a heavy back for strength and a phallic-shaped, hiltless, dark oak handle.

Keeping an ear alert for sounds in the bedroom, I took off my cloak and, soaking a paper towel in warm water, began working on getting the blood out of the shoulder area. Satisfied at last that no more showed, I turned to my jacket and shirt and made sure they were clean as well, then sheathed the knife and returned to the bedroom to check on the girl.

I flinched when I saw only her cloak on the bed, but the shadow standing in a far corner reassured me almost immediately. "Hello," I tried, after taking a deep breath. "You feeling better?"

The girl shrugged and stepped away from the wall. "I'm okay," she answered, her voice guarded.

I glanced at the bed. Several spots of blood showed on the comforter. "You bled a lot. Is your head okay?"

"It hurts," she admitted. "You hit me, didn't you?"

I nodded. "Kicked you, actually. I'm sorry. Your head hit a wall."

"Oh. You won't hit me again, will you?"

I shook my head. "No."

"I'll be fine, then." She started to walk toward the door, hesitated, then suddenly grabbed the arm of an easy chair and sat down. "I'll be fine," she repeated, but she shook her head as she said the words and squeezed her eyes shut several times. "I'll just sit here a bit." She tilted her head back and took a deep breath. "I'll be fine."

I knew she was lying. "Do you have someone—family, perhaps—whom you could call to meet you downstairs?"

She slowly shook her head, then whispered. "They will kill me."

"What? What did you just say?"

"My guardians—the ones who tried to supply you with spiked *naxos* tonight, the ones who ordered me to follow you—they will kill me."

"Why?" I took a seat across from the girl.

"Because," she continued in her low, flat voice. "I could not get your wallet. Madam Sophie took it instead." Her shoulders twitched and she made an open-palmed gesture with her hands but she did not open her eyes. "She wanted me to make sure you did not notice it was gone."

"No!" My hand flew to my hip. The pocket was empty. "Oh, shit." I slumped against the back of the chair and let out a moan as a great sickness began to spread upward from my stomach. "When? How?"

"When she grabbed your arm and showed herself to you." The girl took a deep breath, reached into a pocket in her dress and drew out my wallet and set it on the arm of the chair.

"What?" I grabbed and opened it. Everything, including its paper money, appeared to be still inside. "How'd you get it?"

"Madam Sophie was furious—at you for refusing the third drink, at me for my failure. She yelled at me to follow you and see you kept walking, then come back. I figured, being dead anyways, I'd grab the wallet from the shelf where she had laid it and give it back to you."

I studied the girl for some time, not knowing what I should believe, or what I should do next. How did a girl her age end up in this miserable business?

The whole evening-out idea had seemed like such an easy adventure two hours ago. I knew the language well enough, I knew the city well enough. I had been here for three days and had not seen more than a dozen beggars or panhandlers the many times I had walked the streets. Why would the night be so different from the day? How could a licensed bar—a spirits garden—be dangerous? In this place, I was a grown-up; I could legally drink here. No one treated me like a kid because I was just nineteen.

The first two fillings of the stein had certainly been innocent. The third had smelled different. I had no more than wet my lips and knew it contained something bitter and dangerous. I lifted the stein several times after that, but I had not drunk any of that third filling. I thought I had been smart and clever. Now I had a pickpocketing native girl in my bedroom.

I resolved to start back at my first question. "But why would they kill you?"

The girl sighed. "I was sold to these people. They wanted me to work as a love child, demanded the right to auction me off to the highest bidder. When I understood their plans, I refused their demands. They told me that it was either that or become a remover of wallets. I said I would do that instead. I trained for a month. I have tried six times to make it work. I have only succeeded once. Tonight was my last chance. Tonight, when they get me back, they will start the biddings, and I will die."

Her story sounded so incredibly pathetic I almost refused to believe any of it, except that she obviously was a thief and equally obvious, not a very good one. "How will becoming a prostitute kill you?"

She took another deep breath before answering. "My sister, Nina, was one of their golden girls, the ones you foreigners hear about and come here to enjoy because we are poor and a night with a golden girl is cheap. She got the wasting disease and died three months ago. All the golden girls I know have died of the wasting disease, or have it and soon will. That is why I was willing to try to be a wallet-lifter. I do not want to die."

"But can't you …I mean …" I shut up. What did I really know about this world? I had studied the language and culture for five years, but what I had learned in classrooms or in libraries had dealt with a glorious past—a time of economic and cultural greatness—not this still-devastated reality I discovered when I arrived. I had been in Starnovia for less than two weeks. What did I know? "Does your head still hurt?" I asked, trying to shift to firmer ground.

She nodded.

I got up and touched her scalp. She flinched and pressed her head against the back of the chair. Under the thick hair I could feel a lump as big as a golf ball. "Ugh." I knelt and, grasping both cheeks, gently rotated her head so that I could study her face. The nose, which I had thought large, appeared swollen instead. "Can you breathe out of both nostrils?" I asked.

"Yes," she whispered.

"Okay." I released her head and stood back up. "I think you are going to be okay. Would you like a drink of water? Can I get you anything?"

She shook her head, then opened her eyes. "Do you have a cigarette?"

"No, I'm sorry. I don't smoke."

"Too bad. You Americans have the best cigarettes in the world."

"You shouldn't be smoking at all," I told her.

"Why not? Everyone does."

"Not everybody does. I'll get you some water." I nodded and retreated to the bathroom where I was about to fill one of the hotel glasses when I heard the girl moving about and returned to the bedroom.

She was standing in front of the bureau mirror carefully examining her nose. Catching my reflection, she made a face but did not turn around. She pointed at the bureau top, her gesture taking in my leather-trimmed suitcase and laptop computer case. "You must be a wealthy American to be able to stay here."

I shook my head. "No, just a poor student, actually."

"If you are poor, how rich are your rich?"

"Very rich," I answered.

She turned around, setting her skinny backside against the top of the bureau. "So, why are you here? You tell my guardians you are a scholar. What do scholars do?"

I hesitated. What should I be telling this girl? Shouldn't I be getting her out of here? I could not trust her, so what should I tell her? "I am a student at an American university where I am studying your language and culture. I'm here this summer to take part in an archaeological dig that one of my professors is heading up at Castelschtop outside the town of Mellankos."

"Hmm." The girl's eyebrows went up when I mentioned those names, then she pursed her lips and ran her right hand fingers through her hair. "When will you be going to Mellankos?"

"I …" I hesitated. Any more sharing of information would be stupid. "Soon. I will be returning to Mellankos soon."

Her voice took on a pleading, sad tone. "You are not rich, but you can afford to stay in the Golden Horn. You must have some money. You must have enough to afford to pay an assistant. Is that true?"

Where was this heading? "I have enough funds to cover my expenses this summer. That does not include having an assistant."

She tilted her head and gave me a faint smile. "Not even one who would work for just a few meals and a bed to sleep in?"

I laughed. "I guess I could afford to have an assistant if he was that cheap."

She nodded and smiled. "Good. Then I will go with you as your assistant."

Chapter 3

"What!" I exclaimed. "I can't do that."

"Why not? You just said you could afford an assistant who only worked for meals and a place to sleep."

"No. Look, I'm going to be really busy. I'll be doing a lot of digging and sorting of artifacts. I have to catalog anything we find. It is going to be hot and very dirty. We all just live in tents. It's not going to be any sort of place for a girl whose only schooling is in pick-pocketing!"

"You're mean."

"I'm sorry. I'd like to help you, but Castelschtop just isn't gonna' work." As I said those words, I could feel my wallet pressing against my hip—the wallet she had returned …

Her face twisted and tears began forming. "Please. I don't want to die. I can't go back to the spirits garden!"

"If you start crying, I'll throw you out of here at once." I was tired, feeling cranky and still had the comforter to clean, a shower to take and notes to go over before getting to bed. I wanted her to leave now—while I still had good sense.

Maybe she realized this, for she reduced the tears to sniffles and returned to her chair. She sat in silence for over a minute while I racked my brain trying to figure out how I was to get her out of my room without making a scene.

"Let me help you clean up," she offered. "I have gotten blood out of clothes many times." She pulled the cover off the comforter and, bundling it up, walked with it to the bathroom.

"Please, I can handle this myself," I protested.

"No," she answered. "I have caused this. I will fix it."

I followed her to the bathroom door and stood watching as she turned on the water, struggled a moment to set the temperature, then began rotating the cloth in order to get the first stain under the tap. "Am I doing it right?" she asked.

I hesitated, then nodded.

Keeping an eye on the soaking cover, she picked up a washcloth and began cleaning the dried blood off her face.

The Girl: He was really a nice boy. The men in my village would have called him a boy, even though he was tall and lanky, wore a grown man's knife and had enough soft beard to cover his chin and upper lip. I had a momentary vision of him standing next to Nina, and the two smiling at each other. They would have been perfect for each other. It was a sad thought, and I concentrated once more on my washing. My head still hurt, but my nose felt better. How I longed to scratch it! But I was afraid if I did, the bleeding would start again.

"There. My blood is all gone." I lifted the cover so he could see it was clean. "I also can write a little, and I like to read, and I'm not afraid of snakes or getting my hands dirty. I'm sure I will make you the perfect assistant. I may be thin, but I'm strong. And think of the price? I am so skinny, you could feed me for half of what any of our men would eat."

Suddenly he was laughing. "You are persistent," he said. "Why are you so determined to stay with me?"

"I told you. The ones who bought me from my father are waiting back at the spirits garden. If I go back, they will take me and lock me in a room until a high bidder comes to open me. I know this is so. They auctioned off Tressika last week and last month Irene went the same way. I had to listen to Tressika's screams her first night. Now she struts around like she already knows everything about making love, but I still hear her crying in the mornings when the others are asleep. Soon some ugly man who cares only for his own selfish pleasure will give her the wasting disease. It is her fate. She has told me that the priest in her village read that fate in the soapy waters before she came here. That's why she cries. I cry too, sometimes, but never so loud others hear me."

The scholar nodded. "What did the priest say was going to be your fate?"

I had to take a deep breath before I could answer. "He said my fate was to follow my sister."

"And you say she's dead?"

I nodded. "She stopped writing,. Then the man and woman who bought her came to buy me. Madam Sophie, the one who pickpocketed you tonight and who spiked your drink, she was the one who bought me—she and her husband. She told me Nina had died after I came here."

"Your parents actually sold you—like a donkey, or a cow? And after this Sophie allowed your sister to die?"

"One thousand fifteen *demkoi*! My family will live well for over a year. They will even be able to afford to send my brothers to school. They did not pay as much for me as they did for Nina because I am older." I gave him a sad smile. "When I was still very young, I used to listen to the men praying for children in the church. All they ever asked for was sons—good, strong sons. Not any more. Now they ask for only one son, the rest of the children should be daughters, girls to sell to the cities, playthings for people like you."

The Student: When she ended that little speech, I could not think of what to say. Sure, I had read the stories in *Time* and *The Economist*, but I hadn't thought I would actually meet—face-to-face—one of the so-called "golden girls of Starnovia." Could I, should I, try to save her? Was she being truthful? "Oh, jeez! What am I going to do?"

The girl nodded in an understanding way. "Please, just let me stay here tonight. Master Leo and Madam Sophie won't dare come after me here. You think about it. If it still seems like a bad idea in the morning, I'll leave. Maybe I can find a way out that they won't see me."

"But what if you knife me in the back and take everything while I'm asleep?" I answered.

"You're the one with the knife," she answered.

I touched the dirk and thought about my returned wallet. "Okay. But am I being stupid?"

The girl's eyes grew larger. "No. No, you're being a savior."

Taking turns, we washed up and prepared for bed. When I came out of the bathroom, she was already under the top sheet and comforter on the far side of the bed, her face turned away and her breaths slow and steady. I stared at the carpeted floor. It might not be too bad, except that the bed held the only covers. I gritted my teeth, turned off the light and settled on the near side of the bed. "I'm sleeping with a girl for the first time in my life," I found myself whispering."And I don't even know her name."

Chapter 4

The Girl: The sound of a fork clanging against real china woke me. At first I did not know where I was. Never before had I lain on sheets so smooth, never before had I awakened to smells of freshly-cooked hot bacon, paprika and chives all at the same time. I could see sunlight melting its way through the white curtains, causing them to glow like church altar cloths. I was warm and rested. I did not want to remember yesterday, but I did.

I held still for a long time. Perhaps if I did not move, this heavenly room would stay real. Maybe so, but I felt the need to get up and that was a reality that no fine bed could take away. "Ooh," I finally groaned and stretched until the tips of my toes touched the end of the bed. I rolled over, carefully pulling the comforter with me, then barely opened one eye. He was seated at the room's only table, drinking tea and watching me. I tried a little smile.

He smiled back. "Hello, my little pickpocket. Feeling better?"

I nodded. His hair was a shiny brown, his beard the same except in the middle of the chin where it was blond. He was now wearing glasses, but I could see his eyes were blue. Yes, he would have been perfect for Nina. She was the blue-eyed one. My own eyes are such a mixture that no one ever agrees as to what color they are. When people ask, I say they are golden-green, brown and gray. But when I say that, everyone says I'm just a silly! I propped myself up on one elbow. "Would you hand me my dress? I need to go to the bathroom."

"Sure. Just a moment." He wiped his mouth, got up, and handed my dress to me without quite studying me. You sure are cute— looking away that way, I thought. After all, I still had my slip on. I quickly pulled the dress over my head and retreated to the bathroom.

"Mind if I take a bath?" I called out to him.

"No, go right ahead—provided you don't mind your breakfast getting cold. I already ate my share."

Some of that food was for me? "I'll hurry," I promised.

He had ordered only one breakfast, but it must have been the largest the hotel offered, for there was still plenty of ham and bacon, omelet in the French style and thick slices of our native brown bread. I dug in. I was starting on my third slice of bread when I noticed that he was staring at me and trying not to laugh. "So, what is funny?" I asked.

"This is the girl who last night said that she would not eat nearly as much as a man."

I choked and had to clear my throat and wipe my mouth before I could answer. "I'm sorry. I'll stop now."

"No," he waved away my apology. "Keep eating. It's obvious looking at you that you could use all of this."

I stared at the remaining food. "Are you sure it's okay?"

He nodded. "Absolutely." He leaned back, folding his arms across his chest. "By the way, do you have a name?"

I swallowed. "Jonneanna Marie …Gilenhoff, but everyone just calls me Jonnie."

He nodded. "Jonnie it will be. My name's Jim, Jim Gailey. I'm from Lynn, Massachusetts, over in America." He offered me his right hand.

I cocked one eyebrow and grinned at him before giving him a handshake. "So, do I get to be your assistant?"

"Not so fast, not so fast," he answered. "This is a special dig and everyone who works there needs identification and work papers. Not only that, I'm not even sure my boss will let me use you, even if I can get you in. Maybe it's all right for children your age to work here, but not in America. He's an American too, and he may not want you."

"I'm not a child," I cried. "What am I to do?"

"Hold on, Jonnie. There's no need to cry yet. Let me call Tom Brothers—that's my professor and boss—and ask him." He got up and walked over to his smaller suitcase and began rummaging through it.

"I don't have any papers; I don't have my passbook," I whimpered.

"What?" He turned around to face me, cell phone in hand. "You never had one?"

"No. I have a passbook, but it's still back in the safe at the spirits garden."

He sighed, set down the phone and slid into the nearest chair. "Gad! What are we going to do?" He shook his head several times. "Look, I was going to try to help you, but ...but now I don't see how I can. I was up at the dig the second day I got here. The guards weren't letting anyone near the place without a passbook and a work voucher."

"I didn't know I was going to have to escape last night," I answered.

"What else of yours is back there?" he asked.

"Not much," I told him. "I have two other dresses, some other clothes, a *kabusha* and apron, and my books. I'll miss my books."

Jim was silent so long I found myself counting the ringing of the bells of Saint John's Cathedral. Then he stood up and walked over to the window where he lifted the curtain aside to stare out and down at the streets and rooftops below. I was touching my nose and rubbing my upper arms—hugging myself to keep from crying. For three months I had been telling myself to be tough, to be strong, to stand up to everything and anything this world was going to give me. Now I had a miracle—I had found a boy, an American, who liked me and might even save me, and I didn't have my stupid passbook! "It's not fair!" I screamed, and I started really crying.

My nose started stinging. I sneezed, and he turned around to look at me. "Jonnie? Jonnie, don't. Look, we'll go back to your spirits garden and tell the people there they have to give you your stuff—that's all."

"Oh, you are a crazy American," I sobbed. "They will kill you—and me."

"I don't think so." He smiled. "I hope not. Come on, let's get you cleaned up. I have to be out of this place by noon, so if we're going to get that passbook, we need to do it quickly."

"You are leaving for Mellankos today? How will you get there?"

"I have a Passnobile. It's a piece of crap, worse than a Yugo, but better than a Traubie. It'll get us there. Come on, let's get that pretty face of yours washed and your hair combed. Brush your teeth so that everyone will like your smile."

"I don't have either a toothbrush or a comb."

"Hmm …I thought I saw a packaged comb in the bathroom drawer." Jim went to check. "Ah, yes, here's a comb, still in its sealed wrapper. No toothbrush, but maybe you can rub some paste against your teeth to get them semi-clean."

The toothpaste actually felt good. As for my hair, Jim spent ten minutes combing all the knots out. He was so slow and gentle, he hardly hurt me at all. "This is unbelievable," I told him.

"What? Why?" He paused.

"I've never heard of any man combing a woman's hair. Do all American men do this?"

"Some do." He resumed combing. "How do you want it: braided, ponytails, or just free?"

We could only be headed for trouble. Free hair did not sound like a good idea. "Can you braid it into a single braid—one that hangs down the middle of my back?"

"I can try." He began sorting my hair. "You have very pretty hair—nice and thick," he said. "You still have a goose-egg." He touched it briefly "But it's not as big as last night. How's your nose?"

"Better." I hoped I hadn't broken it, but I couldn't really tell. It still hurt.

"There, all done. Do you have something to fasten it with?"

"Do you have some thread, or a ribbon?"

"How about a shoelace?" he offered. "Would that do?"

"Fine." I took the offered tan lace and quickly fastened the end of the braid. "I guess I'm ready." I stood up and checked myself in the mirror. My eyelids still looked a bit puffy, otherwise I was okay.

Jim: With her hair done, Jonnie looked more civilized and older. Still too skinny for my taste, but maybe a few good meals might help that department. I packed all my bags, and we put on our cloaks. Together we carried everything down to the registration desk, and I signed out. Then we waited for a bellhop to help us move my gear down into the parking garage where I had left the little gray Passnobile I had rented for the summer. No one seemed concerned about Jonnie's presence at all. I locked up the car, and we were ready to take on the spirits garden. At least we were both willing to go there. I do not think either of us felt ready.

The bar was open but had no customers. Inside, the two women who had gotten so friendly with me last night were sitting at a table smoking, a filled ashtray and several dirty steins set between them. A heavy-set man with dark eyes and thick mustache was standing behind the bar counter, wiping glasses. In the background six girls, all teenagers or adolescents, sat grouped in twos at little tables, smoking and watching the three adults and Jonnie and me. I noticed that one of them was missing her left leg from the knee down and another a foot. "Excuse me, are you the proprietor of this place?"

The man straightened and his mouth hardened. He gave me a brief nod.

"I am taking Jonneanna Gilenhoff here with me. We have come to pick up her belongings."

The two women hooted with disbelief; the girls in the background stopped their whisperings. The man picked up something from underneath the counter and laid it on the countertop, covering it with his cleaning cloth. As it clunked on the wooden surface, Jonnie made the slightest hissing sound.

The man smiled in a way that I understood meant he thought me an idiot. "No. Jonneanna must stay here. She may not leave until she has paid off her debt to our business."

"What debt is that?" I asked, although I already had a good idea where this conversation was going.

28

"We have incurred many expenses bringing this girl to the city so that she could get a proper education."

"What would be that total? Huh?"

The man started, then drew his hand away from the cloth-covered object he had been touching. He turned away and pretended to make some calculations. "2036 *demkoi*," he said.

"That's three years wages for any worker! You only paid her father 1015 *demkoi* for her. This is unbelievable!" Angry now, I drew my dirk, hiding it under the cloak.

The man shrugged. "Pay it, or leave her here."

"I should pay you for training her to be a pickpocket and whore? No, you will deliver to us her belongings, including her passbook, and you will do it now!" I yelled. "I will pay you 100 *demkoi*. No more. Otherwise, she still goes with me, but you get nothing."

"Stupid American!" But I drove my dirk through the back of his hand before he could reach the covered object. He screamed, tried to reach the cloth, screamed again and with fluttering fingers knocked a gun, which the cloth had concealed, off the counter. I pressed harder, forcing the knife's tip through his hand and into the counter.

"Now, fat boy, you will tell your lady associates to go to Jonneanna's room and gather up her belongings, all of them, and bring them down here. They will also get her passbook and whatever papers you hold for her. They will do so quickly, and they will not call the police. Otherwise, you can get her things yourself!"

The man grabbed my wrist with his free hand and twisted. I was panting and shaking, but I was not letting go of that knife. I leaned forward and levered his other hand away with my left.

He screamed again and let go of me.

"Leo! Leo, please, we will get the girl's things," Madam Sophie pleaded. I kept my eyes on my enemy but I could hear the two women hurrying out. We waited. No one spoke. I could hear water dripping into the sink behind the bar, the man whimpering every time he moved his blood-covered hand and Jonnie breathing heavily next to me. Otherwise, the room was silent. Only when the sounds of the two women returning reached me, did I feel some hope for an end.

"Here's her suitcase and her clothes; here's her passbook," the one woman said. "We couldn't find her *kabusha*. I don't know where her other shoes are."

"Jonnie, is what you need there?"

I could hear Jonnie moving things around. "Yes, this is enough."

"Good. Pack up the suitcase and close it. Sir, here is your 100 *demkoi*." I dropped a handful of bills on the counter and yanked the knife out. The man groaned and collapsed. "Jonnie, let's go, we have a train to catch for the coast." My eyes swept the room, taking in the two frightened women, the wide-eyed girls and Jonnie—holding a suitcase in one hand, a small semi-automatic pistol in her other. "Oh, my God! Jonnie, put that thing away! Let's go!"

Once we got outside, we both trotted for the hotel. I took the flimsy suitcase from Jonnie, surprised by how light it felt. "I think," I finally managed, "that we had better do some shopping. Not now— when we get to Mellankos. You're going to need more than just two or three dresses."

"I need a *kabusha*," she answered. "If I am to be a grown-up, respectable woman, instead of a pickpocket or whore, I need to cover my hair."

"Here, wear this for now." I took off my brown fedora and set it on her head. "There, now you're respectable."

She giggled, the finest sound I had heard in more than a day, and my heart leaped to hear it. "You are a brave and bold boy," she said. "Is that what makes you a scholar?" She shifted the hat back so that it did not cover her eyes.

"No, but some training in martial arts helps."

"You must teach me sometime. I want to be able to pin a man's hand to a counter too."

"I don't think so. He could have shot both of us. Speaking of which: what did you just do with his gun?"

"I put it in my suitcase."

"Oh?" I hesitated, then decided now was not the time to worry about it.

We reached the car without incident and got in. As I fastened my seatbelt, my energy drained away as suddenly as if I were an electrical motor and someone had just pulled the plug. I felt dead tired and even sick in the stomach now. I closed my eyes, remembering …I had actually stabbed a man, threatened his life— for what, for whom? A girl I barely knew? Was I going crazy? I took a deep breath and tried to get the key into the ignition, fumbling and missing the slot several times before managing to get the key and the hole lined up. "Jonnie," I whispered. "I feel for shit."

"Jim?"

"What?"

"Thank you for saving my life. Can we go to Mellankos now?"

"Yes." I took a deep breath and turned the key.

Part II: Mellankos

Chapter 5

From Noviastad to the ancient city of Mellankos was 100 kilometers over the best road in Starnovia. The land mines had come out of the roadbed three years ago, and NATO peacekeepers cleared out the shoulders to a distance of ten meters a year later. The concrete still needed some patching, but the bridges were new. The trip took just over an hour.

I asked Jonnie a lot of questions during that hour and she answered all of them. Her stories were consistent and I believed mostly truthful, although she often sat silently for some time before answering.

Her father, she told me, had been a furniture maker before the war; her mother a sewing machine operator. They were both of the more Germanic Plokan people and belonged to the Lutheran Church, an ethnic and religious group dominant in parts of the north but a minority in her own village. She had one older brother. He had been drafted into the army and died in the war. She still had two younger brothers, now ages six and nine. When the rebels attacked their village, Jonnie and her family hid in caves east of the town for five days. After the rebels withdrew, they returned home to find her father's shop had been destroyed along with half their house. He lost all his tools and wood and had been unable to work since. The clothing factory had burned as well. Her mother now did laundry in the river by hand for less than a *demkos* a day. Jonnie had gone to school until the war started. The rebels destroyed the schoolhouse. The government promised a new building, but so far no construction had started. A few private schools were operating but only the richer could afford to send their children.

I listened to her story, shaking my head occasionally, but keeping my eyes out for the local pickup trucks and motor scooters that would whip by without warning every other minute. Here were three ethnic groups and three religions crammed into a tiny country with a history of sectional hatred—and part of a culture steeped in vendetta and honorable revenge. As Dr. Brothers said, here nobody forgets anything or forgives anyone. I, myself, was on some spirits garden owner's permanent shitlist without any doubt at all. The sadder side of this old tale was that the Starnovians had a past rich in music, poetry and dance and once, back in the 17th Century, they had united to fight as one against the Turks. The story of their ultimately futile struggle, ending in the siege of Castelschtop, was one of the great epic stories of European history—one filled with heroism, sacrifice and, in the end, betrayal. If they had acted as one people then, why couldn't they act that way now in the Twenty-first Century?

In that hour of driving we moved from the more Germanic north into the more Slavic south. As we traveled, the number of ruins in the villages increased, and the land took on an increasingly neglected feel. The farms I saw near Noviastad had horses, machinery and healthy-looking cattle, and the fields were green and well cared for. The smell of fresh manure and Starnovia's famous roses hung in the air everywhere. South of the Molar River, I saw few fields under cultivation and the land smelled only of dust. The people we passed appeared thin with hollow cheeks and grim faces. Many, including children, were getting about on crutches, victims of the mines still plentiful in the countryside. The heaviest fighting had taken place in the south. Now these villages were exporting girls to the north in return for enough *demkoi* to feed the survivors.

The city of Mellankos put on a better appearance. All the streets were clear of rubble. Farm wagons with fresh produce lined the curbs and people were buying. A few of the houses boasted new glass and roof tiles. Jonnie rolled down her window and peered out with open curiosity. I felt my own spirits lift, and they improved even more when I turned into the Antiquities Institute's lot and saw three new Land Rovers with the Department's logo painted on their doors parked in front. The building sported fresh, clean white paint and the Starnovian and United Nations flags fluttered together by the entrance. "We need to go in here first before going out to Castelschtop," I explained to Jonnie. "I need to see if Dr. Brothers is here, so we can get you your work permit."

Jonnie shrugged and gave me a smile. "Sounds fine," she said. She put my hat back on her head and followed me inside.

The place had no air conditioning, and the two overhead fans in the stuffy main lobby were not running. A dog kept barking and a dozen people, mostly men in working clothes, clogged the hallways. Taking Jonnie's arm, I guided her through the crowd until we reached Brothers' office. I knocked on the closed door and sighed with relief to hear a cheerful American-accented voice call out "If you're here about getting a job, you have the wrong door."

"It's Jim Gailey, Tom. I think I already have a job."

"Oh, Jim! Come in, come in!" I opened the door and, waving Jonnie ahead of me, entered my boss's office.

The high-ceilinged room stank of stale coffee grounds and cigarette smoke—the same way it had the last time I had visited. Except for the keyboard and mousepad of Tom's computer, papers and printouts covered every inch of the old oak desk. Tom was seated in a battered wooden office chair, feet propped on the nearest windowsill, an ash-loaded cigarette in his right hand, his bald head reflecting the late morning sun. He squinted a moment through his bifocals at Jonnie before giving his wispy gray beard a few strokes and chuckling. "Who you got with you, Jimmy? Your younger sister?"

The other person in the room turned to stare at both of us. I had never seen her before, but I guessed she was probably the third American student Tom had said he was expecting. Certainly her loose, tan polo shirt, bluejeans and brown hair barretted and scrunchied in a single ponytail all spoke of an American background.

I nodded to the newcomer. "Hi, I'm Jim Gailey, one of Tom's students. This is Jonneanna Gilenhoff. She's going to be my assistant."

Tom snorted. "Assistant? My ass! Where'd you dig *her* up?" He shook his head. "Jim, you're worse than Bob Covert. He arrived yesterday with an 'assistant' too—only he introduced her as his 'consultant'. She, at least, was twenty. How old's this one?"

Jonnie must have sensed the drift of our conversation—even if she could not understand the words—for she drew herself up straight, lifted off my hat in a salute and looked Tom directly in the eye. "I am here to help Scholar Jim any way I can. I can read and I can write. As for computers, I can learn. I'll not be a burden, I promise." She sighed and her voice faltered. "Please, I'll not cause you any trouble."

Tom studied her, then laughed again and leaned forward far enough to shake her hand. "Well, you're a bold one. How old are you?" he asked in her language.

"Sixteen years and two months, sir," she answered. I started and stared at her. I would have guessed fourteen—absolute max. If she was sixteen, she was a lot older than she looked.

"Hello, Jonneanna," the woman said in clear, barely-accented Starnovian. "I'm Sondra Mikmosser. I'm an American student here for the summer like Jim." She offered a slender, almost delicate hand to Jonnie who studied it, smiled and shook it firmly.

"Pleased to meet you, Ma'am," she said to Sondra. "Where in America are you from?"

"San Francisco, big city on the west coast in California."

"Well," Tom interrupted, speaking in Starnovian. "Jim, I'll tell you the same thing I told Bob Covert yesterday. We can't pay her a single *demkos*, but if Jonneanna's willing to work, I can make room for her to sleep and can spare enough food for three meals a day. Understand?"

Jonnie nodded. "That's the way Jim told me it would be."

Tom's eyebrows went up. "He did? Huh. Well, I guess there's no negotiating to do, is there?" He turned to me. "Jimmy, please, a minute with you alone." He lowered his feet to the floor, stubbed out his cigarette and led the way to the door. "Sondra, I'll get back to you on the south wall project in a moment. Jonnie, please wait with Sondra, would you."

"Yes, Dr. Tom," Jonnie said.

Outside, Tom closed his office door and signaled for me to follow him out of the building and to the backyard. When we reached the other side of a storage shed that hid us from the headquarters, he stopped and turned around. "Jim, she's a whore, and she's a child! I thought that you, of all my students, would have more sense than to bring one of these children to this place."

"Tom, she's not a whore! Honest."

"So how did you meet her then?"

"In a spirits garden."

Tom snorted. "I met her 'in a spirits garden', but she's 'not a whore!'" Those two statements together are the craziest, oxymoronic combination I've ever heard!" Tom paused and sighed. "Okay, okay. I gave Bob a break with his little sexpot; I'll give you a break too." He rubbed his forehead and walked in a circle. "She's a child! Okay. You heard my offer in the office—it stands. It's against my better judgement, and it's not a lot, but I know that half the people in this country are beggin' for any work at all. And I know a lot of these girls don't want to be prostitutes, but ..." He paused and looked me in the eye. "I will not hire her, or even allow her in camp, if she has any kind of health problems at all. Understand?"

I took a deep breath. "I'm pretty sure she's safe, but I see your point."

"Good. When we get back to the office, I'll give you the name and address of a doctor here in Mellankos. She's under contract with the Antiquities Institute. You will take Jonneanna to this doctor this afternoon and have her give Jonnie a complete physical. If she's clean, I guess we can let her in. But, otherwise, put her on a bus back to Noviastad immediately. Understand?"

"Yes, sir."

"Good. I'm telling you this because we simply can't afford to have even one case of the clap or anyone showing HIV-positive at the end of this summer. My ass would be grass, and so would this entire program." He sighed. "That girl Bob came with ... You would not believe her. Well, maybe you would. Boobs just about busting right out of her dress and talk about all over him! She was nibbling his ear and rubbing his neck. Poor boy was havin' a hard time keeping it in his pants the whole time we were talking. Fortunately she was clean. If she hadn't of been, I would have had to get him checked and probably would have shipped him home too."

"Yes, sir." What else was I to say?

"Another thing, please don't get any ideas about taking her home with you in August. I have enough headaches with this project as it is. Oh, and get yourself a supply of prophylactics. Or are my dirty-old-man instincts wrong?"

I shook my head. "No. I'm okay. I don't think I'll need them. I'll take her to that doctor now. Got to go do some shopping anyway."

"What do you need? Maybe we already have it."

"Jonnie needs shoes, other clothes and she wants a *kabusha*."

Tom pursed his lips in surprise. "She wants to wear a *kabusha*? Huh. Maybe she's as old as she claims—and as respectable as you claim. That would be a first. Well, good luck. I'll let you go." He started back toward the building, fumbling inside his shirt pocket. "Damn! Where'd I put my cigarettes?" He shrugged. "Maybe I left them on my desk."

Chapter 6

"Sondra, do you see my cigarettes anywhere?"

My colleague looked up as Tom and I came back in the office. "No, I don't see them. Didn't you have them in your shirt pocket?"

Tom shrugged. "I could have sworn I did. Well, who knows?" He resumed his seat and sighing, flipped through papers and looked in his desk drawers in a vain attempt to spot his pack. "Damn. Well, don't let me keep you, Jim. You've your marching orders. Here's a medical form and here's the name of the physician and the address. I think it's the only building on the block in good enough shape for occupancy." He looked underneath his desk and behind his chair, then at me. "Oh, one more thing: where's she going to sleep?"

"Huh? I hadn't thought about that."

"If you tell me you're just treatin' her like a sister and want a separate tent for her, first, I won't believe you, but second, I'll have to figure out if such a place even exists. Not even sure we have any free tents. If you say 'I'll take care of her', well, you have your own tent, just like Bob. I can find a spare bed and have it moved into your tent before you even get up there tonight. You'll lose half your space, but that's your problem."

"Shit," I whispered. "That doesn't sound like a choice, really." I glanced at Jonnie, who was looking confused.

"It isn't," Tom replied. "I just thought I'd ask in order to soften the blow a bit, so to speak."

"Jim? Tom? If Jonnie needs a place to sleep, she can tent with me," Sondra volunteered.

"Would you? But that's not fair to you." I said.

"Don't worry about me," Sondra answered. "I think Jonneanna will do fine. And I think it would be a better arrangement for everyone." She gave Jonnie a smile.

Tom and I both nodded. "Yes, you're absolutely right."

Jonnie shrugged. "Any place you want me is fine."

"Okay. I'll phone and have a bed put in Sondra's tent then." Tom looked much happier then he had earlier. "Okay. See you two in a little bit. Oh. Grab a lunch in the canteen on your way out. Wait, here's a slip for Jonneanna to get something too. She's so thin, she looks ready for the wind to pick her up and float her to Russia. Supper's here at six. See me before then, and if things have gone well, I'll have a voucher card for Jonneanna. What was your last name again?"

"Gilenhoff, sir," Jonnie answered.

"Hmm, a royal name with a long, glorious past. Okay, git." Tom waved us out and turned to Sondra.

"See you later, Tom. Nice to meet you, Sondra, and—and, thanks a lot." I waved back, and Jonnie and I left.

We both picked up sandwiches and bottles of warm ginger beer and headed out to the car. I explained what had to happen as we went. Jonnie nodded. "Will the doctor look at all of me and poke me?"

"Probably. He may even give you some inoculations."

"Oh." Except for sounds of her eating, Jonnie was quiet the rest of the short trip down the cobbled main street to the central plaza—with its still-intact but silent, waterless fountains—and over to a side street corner where I parked. The doctor's building, stuccoed in tan and cream in the traditional style and sporting a new metal roof, stood alone on the corner. Where another building to the right should have been, a plank fence partially concealed a hole. On the opposite corner, a bakery still stood, but its metal, roll-down shutters were closed and all the upper story windows were broken. An eight or nine year old boy sat on a tiny stool by the curb, bunches of Starnovian roses surrounding him, their gay reds and yellows a solitary happy note. He pushed his hair away from his forehead when Jonnie and I got out of the car and gave us a game wave. A patch covered where his left eye should be, and most of the fingers of his left hand were missing. I remembered the girls back in the spirits garden with missing leg and foot and the others we had seen in route. What land mine had gotten this kid? I wondered. One of the bright, colorful plastic ones that look like toys but blow up in a child's hand? I smiled at the boy, but reluctantly did not buy. "Later, friend," I told him, and directed Jonnie toward the door with the sign for the doctor's office.

"Good day, Ma'am," I greeted the nurse-receptionist seated behind a desk. "I have hired Jonnie Gilenhoff here to be my assistant for the Antiquities Institute's project at Castelschtop. She needs a physical as a condition of employment." I signed to Jonnie to show the woman her paperwork. Was I doing this right, saying the right words?

The nurse, a sad-eyed, older woman in stained but clean whites and with a brown *kabusha* tied over her hair, nodded and took the papers and Jonnie's passbook. Her eyebrows lifted only briefly as she read the information in the passbook. "Be seated," she said when she had finished reviewing the papers.

One of the room's three hardwood benches had space for two, and Jonnie and I sat down together. The other four people in the room looked up then turned their faces away. Outside I could hear vehicles drive by and the shouts of children playing. Inside, a mantel clock ticked on a shelf above the nurse's desk, and an old man seated on one of the other benches cleared his throat—otherwise the room was wrapped in quietness. I took several deep breaths, savoring the reassuring odors of alcohol and pine oil. The place was clean. I started on my own sandwich, chewing as quietly as I could.

We sat in this dull silence for ten minutes, then a woman left and the nurse called the man with the throat congestion into a back room. After he had gone in, Jonnie gripped my arm and her voice quivered. "Jim? Jim, I'm scared."

"Huh? Why? You've been to a doctor before, haven't you?"

"No."

"No? Didn't you have to get some shots before you started school?"

"Yes, but the village nurse came to the school and gave them. Jim, what's he going to do to me?"

"He'll check you over. Probably take a sample of your blood and urine and run tests on them. It's just a physical. I had to have one before I came over here."

She let go of my arm. Glancing at her, I could see that she was slowly rubbing her hands together, as if she were working in hand cream.

Jonnie gave me one brief, fear-filled glance when the nurse called her name, then walked through the doorway to the far room where I could see another woman waiting. Woman? I rechecked the directions Tom Brothers had given me. Yes, the doctor was a woman. "Well, I hope that helps," I said to myself. It would be even better if Jonnie was in perfect health.

Half-an-hour later, that same woman came out to the front room, looked around and motioned for me to join her. "Hello. You are Master Gailey, yes? I am Dr. Fessenoff. Jonneanna is to be your assistant, I understand?"

I nodded. "Yes. She's all right?"

The doctor gave me a reassuring smile. "She's fine. She's getting dressed and will be out in a minute. Ah …" She paused and glanced away.

"Jonnie's all right?"

"Yes. She's healthy, no disease, and she's not pregnant. Tsk …I do have one concern though." She looked me in the eye. "You see how thin she is? Many, many of our children are growing up slowly now because of poor nutrition. She will grow; she still has time. But …and this is where my concern lies. Jonneanna, like so many of our children, has been forced to grow up too quickly. I mean, mentally she is an adult, or mostly so, and acts that way, but physically, she's an adolescent. I do not know what your intentions with her are, but …" Her eyes searched my face. "You do understand me?"

"Doctor, I don't think that is my plan …"

"Good. Then perhaps I was needlessly concerned, but you will remember?"

"Yes, I will." I gave the doctor a slight bow.

"Oh," Dr. Fessenoff added. "Her nose? It is broken, but it'll be fine. She must just be careful she does not bump it again soon. Okay?"

"Okay."

The back room door opened, and Jonnie, smiling now, rejoined me. "I'm ready to go," she said.

I signed some paperwork so that the Institute would pay for the visit, and we left. Returning to the car, I stopped and bought a red rose from the boy.

He gave me a brave smile and whispered blessing along with the flower.

"God, I can't save everyone," I told myself as I walked away. "What am I to do here?" I laid the rose on the back seat of my car and got in.

"Ready to go shopping?" I asked Jonnie as I pulled back onto the street.

"Ah-huh."

"How'd it go in there?"

"Fine. Doctor was very nice. She explained what and why she was doing everything. She said it was nice to have a patient who was clean. She did poke at me, but she was gentle, and it wasn't so bad. The worse part was when she pricked my finger to get blood. That hurt!"

"I bet it did."

"Oh, and she gave me two shots. They hurt too. One for tetanus, one for typhoid. Is that right?"

"Sounds right," I answered. "So, what do we need first? Ah, let's try here." I slowed, spotted a parking space half-a-block ahead and pulled in.

"What did you see? Where are we going?" Jonnie asked, looking around.

"Cobbler shop back there. You'll need work shoes if you're going to be on the dig. Sandals won't cut it."

Jonnie: Jim first took me to a shoemaker's. He asked the deskman to fit me with work boots such as the diggers at the Castelschtop site were wearing. At first, the man looked at me and laughed, but when Jim pulled out his wallet, the man turned serious and instructed me to come around to his display room where he had chairs and stools for fitting. Setting several pairs of brown, heavy-soled, high-topped, leather boots in front of me, he took out a footstick and measured my right foot. He shook his head. "These are the smallest sizes I have pre-made," he said, "and your foot is a size smaller than any of these."

"Perhaps Jonnie will be growing. Let's try the smallest size with heavy socks," Jim suggested.

The deskman shrugged and fetched several pairs of flecked gray, woolen socks. We found a pair of socks that fit, and he put the shoes on my feet. I stood up and walked around the room as I remembered I should from times before the war when my mother used to take Nina and me shoe shopping. Nina had always gotten new shoes; Momma never made her wear my castoffs. These boots had rubber lug soles and stiff, heavy, leather uppers. I could feel the shoes cutting into parts of my feet, but they were certainly long enough and wide enough. They were too big, but I smiled and nodded anyway. "Yes, these fit well enough."

The next stop was the big market. Many of the food vendors had already left since it was by now mid-afternoon, but the other merchants were still at their stalls. Jim took me to a stand where a man was offering piles of socks, underwear, tee-shirts and other clothes he claimed all had come from Germany or Italy. I was not so sure. Many items looked like Bulgarian or Serbian manufacture, but we found three pairs of socks I liked, some underwear that did not feel too scratchy, slips, tee-shirts and two pairs of trousers made of heavy cotton denim—like the jeans Jim was wearing, but cut in the Starnovian fashion and therefore, not worth nearly as much. Jim also found me two long-sleeved shirts and, at another stand, a wide selection of *kabushas*. "Here's what you've wanted," he said, directing my attention to the colorful display.

"Oooh, yes." I reached out and touched *kabushas* printed with roses—many, many roses—and spring flowers and grape and olive leaves. "These are so beautiful."

"Get what you want," Jim said.

I took a deep breath and held it. I was to be an assistant, a worker. I was not to be a Sunday showpiece. I let out my breath and turned to the plain colored *kabushas* lying off by themselves. "I am to be a worker; I must wear a worker's colors," I said. I picked out two black kabushas, one of which was decorated with tiny stars, and a dark brown one. "These …these are all I need."

The old woman tending the stall gave me a sad, toothless, but sympathetic smile. "You do not wish for the red or yellow?"

I shook my head. "No, I must be grown up now and wear a woman's colors. Besides, the black will not show the dirt as easily."

"You're wise," she said, starting to wrap the three *kabushas* carefully in newspaper.

"Add this one to the purchase," Jim suddenly put in. He lifted off one of the printed *kabushas* from the display and, folding it carefully, added it to my selections. It was royal blue in background color, overlaid with golds and dark pink roses. It was the most beautiful *kabusha* in the stall, the one I had immediately looked at, the one I had known I would be dreaming of that night. My mouth fell open, but I could not speak.

Chapter 7

"That is *indeed* a lovely one," the stallkeeper admitted. "Fit for a princess. I cannot let it go for less than ten *demkoi*."

"Hmm." Jim studied the *kabusha*. I could feel my own lips quivering with desire. He smiled at the woman. "I would agree that no one could dream of selling this work of art for less than ten *demkoi*. That is a modest price for one of such beauty. But, I'm sure you would agree that the others my assistant has selected are but a shadow of its value. Therefore, I am sure you will not be offended when I tell you that I will pay eleven *demkoi* for all four."

The woman laughed. "You are a shrewd man. Twelve *demkoi* and all are yours."

Jim looked her straight in the eyes. "You are a hard bargainer, and I am beggaring myself. Eleven and a half—ten for the *kabusha* of beauty and half a *demkos* for each of the other three."

The woman pressed her lips together, but then she smiled and nodded vigorously.

I felt so full of joy and surprise at that moment that all I could do was stare at Jim's choice. Only the Maid of May in our village had ever worn such a *kabusha* as that one. It was this vender's display piece, the one to draw shoppers to her stand, the one she would never have dreamed of selling in a month of years. Ten *Demkoi*! That was as much money as my mother earned in three weeks!

It was at that moment that I saw Jim as someone for myself, and not as someone for Nina. He had saved my life, and now he had given me the gift of a lifetime. What man in all Starnovia would have done either of those things for one such as myself?

Back in the car, I sat staring at the fancy *kabusha*, stroking it, still not believing its reality. "Thank you," I whispered. I lifted Jim's fedora off my head and put it carefully back on his. Then, taking one of the black *kabusha*, I wrapped the large triangle of cloth around my forehead and secured the two long ends in a knot underneath my braid in the back. Now my head finally felt right. I squeezed myself with pleasure before repacking the others and laying the bundle on the backseat. "What else?" I asked.

"Pharmacy, if Mellankos has one."

It did. Many shelves were bare, and the attendants were rude and lazy, but we did find a toothbrush, some soap, a towel and washcloth. Jim paid for these items too. As we were leaving, he spotted a shop with a few pieces of old furniture and other antiquities in it. "This looks interesting. I think I'll check it out. You want to come in too?"

"I will wait here," I said.

I thought he would be in the store maybe five, even ten minutes. I turned my back and lit up, but I had taken no more than two drags when I heard the store door slam, and Jim was walking toward me. "Jonnie?"

I cupped the cigarette in my hand and rotated my body to conceal it. "What? Oh, you surprised me."

"Jonnie."

"Yes?"

"Show me your hand. No, your other hand." His voice had turned steel-hard—like he had sounded when talking to Master Leo. "Jonnie, where did you get an American cigarette?"

"American cigarette?"

"Look, you little pickpocket, don't try to bullshit me! Do you understand? I can tell the difference between an American cigarette and a French, or a Turkish one at ten feet by smell alone. You took Dr. Brothers' cigarettes right out of his pocket when he introduced himself. Yes?"

I stared at the pavement, wondering if, at that moment, it would open up and swallow me. I almost wished it would. "Yes," I whispered.

"I can't afford to have a thief, someone I can't trust, sharing Sondra's tent, working with me." His voice twisted, as if he were trying not to cry. "I think there's still one bus to Noviastad tonight. Can you think of any reason why I shouldn't just put you on it?"

I flicked the ash off the end of the cigarette and, wetting my fingers, killed the live part. Taking the pack out of my pocket, I shoved the butt back in with the others. I stared at the red and white box—Marlboro, American cigarettes—then without looking up I offered the pack to Jim. "I'm sorry," I managed.

I knew I was starting to cry. Oh, please, please don't let the tears show! He doesn't like tears. I held the pack out to him for a long time, but he did not take it. My arm grew tired. Finally, I had to lower it. When I raised my eyes, Jim was still standing there, looking at me. "I'm sorry," I said again.

"Jonnie, get in the car." Jim ordered. I did. He got in his side, fastened his seatbelt and started the car. Without a word, he put it in gear and we drove off. Five minutes later I could see the bus terminal up ahead. Jim slowed and pulled into the nearest space. I knew then that it was too late. I had everything: a safe job, a future, an American willing to buy me anything, even willing to risk his life for me. I had thrown it away. For what? An American cigarette. Still, I sat up straight, the half-crushed box still in my hand, and waited. I could not cry now—I could not even pray—but I would be strong.

I knew Jim was looking at me. Why didn't he order me out of the car? What was he waiting for? "Jonneanna?"

I jumped." Yes?" I whispered as soon as I could settle my heart.

Jim sighed. "I'm going to give you a choice."

I nodded, breath held.

"You can get out now. In which case, you get to keep the cigarettes, and I'll buy you a one-way ticket to Noviastad. Or, you can stay in the car. If you stay, I'll drive you back to the Institute's building. When we get there, you'll get out and go inside to Dr.

Brothers' office. You'll return his cigarettes to him. Wait, I'm not done. You will tell him you took them, and you will apologize. If, after you apologize, he tells you that you may stay, I'll let you work for me. Understand?"

I slowly nodded.

His voice softened. "What will it be?"

I stared at the cigarette pack, wondering now why I had thought myself so clever taking it, and wondering how I thought I was going to be able to smoke any of them without Jim or everyone else knowing. Seeing them made me feel stick in my stomach. I certainly didn't want them. "You take them. I don't want them," I tried.

"No, Jonnie. You have to take them back yourself to Dr. Brothers."

"But once he knows, he won't want me either." I pleaded.

Suddenly, I felt Jim's hand resting on my arm. "If you don't do it, I will never trust you again. And if I can't trust you, you might as well get out right now and head for that bus."

"Oh, Jim, you're not fair! You know Dr. Brothers won't let me stay once he knows I took his cigarettes." I had told myself to be strong, but here I was sobbing. "You want me on that bus; you want to get rid ...of ...me." My words trailed off. I was about to say that he was just pretending to give me a choice, but now I was remembering that beautiful *kabusha* he had just bought for me, and I knew that thought was wrong. I was the rotten apple in the bowl. Jim, Dr. Tom, Sondra, the doctor, everyone I had met had been honest and nice, even gone out of their way for me. "I'm sorry." I started wiping my eyes. "I'll go back. I'll return the cigarettes. I'm sorry I took them. I will never take anything again!" I pulled the fourth plain *kabusha*, the lighter and the extra underwear I had taken in the market out from under my cloak and lay them beside the cigarettes.

"What?" Suddenly Jim was laughing. "Jonnie, you're incredible! And I've been telling myself that you weren't a good pickpocket." He turned on the ignition, backed the car out of its space and headed it toward the Institute's building.

It was not yet 5 o'clock when we got back there. "Here," he said, handing me the paperwork the doctor had filled out. "Take these to Tom as well. If he forgives you, he'll want these."

I nodded. "Thank you." I got out and, leaving the rest of my loot on the seat, carried the cigarettes into the building. The crowds were gone from the hallway and only one tall, sloped-shouldered man was still standing in the hall waiting when I knocked on the office door.

"Who's there?"

"Dr. Brothers? It's Jonnie Gilenhoff."

"Jonnie? Oh, Jonneanna? Yes. Come in."

Dr. Brothers was in exactly the same position I had last seen him earlier—feet propped up, leaning back in his chair. The difference this time was that he was holding a pencil in one hand and slowly rotating and fondling it. "How'd it go at the doctor's?" he asked.

"Fine, sir. I brought the papers she filled out." I offered the forms, and he took them.

"Ah, good. Where's Jim?"

"He's waiting outside. Sir?"

Dr. Brothers held up a finger as a sign to wait as he started reading over the forms. His eyebrows went up twice, and he nodded. "Good. Excellent. Good. This certainly restores my faith in Jim's judgment." He got up and opened the top drawer of a filing cabinet where he placed the medical form in a folder, then pulled out several other forms. "Well, let's get a job voucher and a meal pass filled out for you so you can draw rations, so to speak, and get on site."

"Sir?"

"Yes, Jonneanna?"

"You …you look as if you could use a cigarette."

Dr. Brothers stared at the pencil still in his right hand and laughed. "You know, you're right. But I lost the pack I had, and the rest are at camp. I guess I'm just going to have to wait 'til I get back there tonight."

I set the pack on his desk. "Here they are."

"What?" Dr. Brothers stared at the pack, picked it up, shook it and dropped out one cigarette—which turned out to be the one I had started. He studied it a moment, then looked me in the eye.

"I took them. I'm sorry. I only used that one a little bit."

"You took them? How? They were in my shirt pocket!"

I shrugged. "I guess ...I just did. I'm sorry. I won't do it again." For a moment Dr. Brothers looked as if he were going to be angry, so I hurried on with my speech. "I know what I did was wrong. Jim said that he should send me back to Noviastad. But he said my only other choice was to take the cigarettes back to you and apologize. That's what I'm doing, because I really do want to work here and be a good helper, and I really like Jim and you and Sondra. Please, I promise I will never take anything from anybody again, and I promise I won't ever, ever smoke another cigarette either. Please?"

Suddenly Dr. Brothers was laughing. "Enough! Enough. Jim told you that you had to return the cigarettes and apologize?"

"Yes ..."

"Well, son-of-a-goatherder. You're something else, Miss Gilenhoff." He was still chuckling. "Apology accepted. Let me get your paperwork done, and I'll let you out of here. Do you have your passbook?" I got it out of the pocket inside my cloak and handed it to him. He cleared just enough space to write, opened the passbook and began copying out information from it onto the forms. Someone knocked. "Come in," Dr. Brothers called without looking up.

Jim entered and took a seat beside me. "So, how'd it go?"

"I guess I get to stay," I felt weak and tired.

Jim nodded. "Good."

Dr. Brothers looked up. "Jim, you told me that Jonneanna here wasn't involved with the spirit garden's main business. What you didn't tell me is she's the best pickpocket in Starnovia."

"Sorry, Tom. That's sort of how we met."

"I thought you picked her up in a spirits garden."

"I did. She was the joint's pickpocket-in-training. I caught her in the act."

"So she's not as good as she appears?"

"Not at getting wallets out of pants, anyway."

"So, what's going to happen?" Tom asked.

"You tell him, Jonnie," Jim ordered.

"I told you. My pickpocketing days are over. I promised Jim, and I'll promise you, I'll never take anything that isn't mine ever again."

"Okay." Dr. Brothers stood up. "Jonnie—that's what you call yourself?—here's your job voucher and meal pass. Keep them with your passbook, or some place safe. Or, is this like the question of who shaves the barber? Who would steal from the pickpocket?" He laughed. "I think I'm done here. You guys want to eat an early supper with me so you can head up to camp and get there in time to get settled?"

"Sure," Jim answered. "Sounds good."

"Okay." Dr. Brothers gestured out and followed us into the hallway, locking the door to his office before leading the way to the dining room-canteen and kitchen at the other end of the building.

Part III: Castelschtop

Chapter 8

We left Mellankos just after six, convoying behind Dr. Brothers, who was driving one of the Institute's Land Rovers. When the road turned to rutted dirt and gravel, Jim slowed, letting Dr. Brothers get ahead. "Love these roads," he commented. "If the land mines don't get you, the dust will."

He was treating me again as he had in the morning. I guessed maybe supper had helped. Jim and Dr. Brothers certainly told me enough stories about good times and bad, perhaps more for my benefit than theirs.

As we drew closer to Castelschtop, I found myself peering through the dirty windshield more and more, looking forward to my first glimpse of the place that is my country's most sacred place, the location of the saddest moment in our history …

When the Turks came to the Balkans, defeating first the Bulgarians, then the Serbs, Transylvanians and finally the Hungarians, Starnovia, fast in its own mountains, had been left alone. Only after their defeat in the siege of Vienna did the great Turkish horde turn its attention to my country. When their vanguards tried to enter the lowlands, the people rallied to King Stephen's call. Almost every able-bodied man and youth in the country turned out. We were many, but ill-equipped and without discipline or training. Ten thousand died in the battle of the Crystal Pass before the Turks pushed their way into and through the low-lying north country. They burned Noviastad then moved south, killing those who resisted, destroying those villages and towns that tried to deny them entry. The king and his family and our few remaining trained soldiers retired before the onslaught until they reached Castelschtop. There King Stephen resolved to take his stand and, in preparation, sent for the golden horn.

What our horn actually looked like no one remembered. The mark of the Golden Horn Hotel in Noviastad showed something that looked like a bugle, but my music teacher in church said that it probably looked like a hunting horn with a wide bell and large coils that a person could carry under one's arm. That is the kind of horn that appears on my country's flag. Our legends described it as being made of pure gold—although not even my youngest brother believed that. Three times before our kings had ordered the horn to be blown. Each time, the country had united and come forward successfully to destroy our enemies.

King Stephen sent out word that when the horn would be blown, everyone was to join in one last battle for the future of our land. My teachers said that he hoped to lure the Turks into a siege and then trap them between his own troops and his people. If that was the plan, the Turkish army took the bait, massing around Castelschtop and bringing up huge cannons and building great earthworks and ditches. The people armed themselves as best they could and waited for the sound of the famous horn.

The horn never blew. After days of waiting, the bravest men approached Castelschtop to find it occupied by the Turks who were busy knocking down the last walls. Word went out that everyone, even the king's family, had died fighting. None had surrendered. None had been spared. No one knew why the horn had not been blown.

But then new rumors started to come out of the Turkish camps. A Starnovian from the south, a man of Slavic background, had been the horn blower. He had gotten the order to blow the horn, but, having taken a bribe from the Turks, he fled the fortress via a little used postern gate instead and took the horn with him. The Turks soon got in that gate and, taken by surprise, the defenders never had a chance.

"Trustworthy as a Starnovian Slav" was an expression I could remember hearing from the time I was a baby. Everyone knew what it meant; everyone knew the particular Slav the remark referred to. The betrayal broke our country. Almost two hundred years were to pass before the Turks left, and in all that time, my countrymen fought each other more than the Turks, until, even as our latest civil war proved, no one ever seemed to trust anyone.

Now I was going to be part of the new order—a worker in the dig that our new president had ordered. His enemies were complaining that it was a waste of what little funds Starnovia had. His friends described it as a way to once more give my country a common focus. I did not know myself. It had been hard to think about politics when staying alive was the first priority. Now I found myself thinking about nothing else. I gripped the door handle and could not keep myself from grinning in anticipation.

But when Castelschtop finally came into view, I had to admit disappointment. It appeared to be little more than a white and green mound covered with trees and surrounded by a high, wired fence. Even the hill it stood on did not look impressive. Maybe, I told myself, maybe once we get inside, there'll be more to see.

Jim: We caught up with Tom at the gate. Jonnie and I showed the guard our paperwork and he waved us through. Tom turned right in order to return the Land Rover to the car pool. I turned left and headed for the foreign nationals housing.

The Starnovian government was paying half the expenses of the dig. UNESCO and several American foundations were paying the rest. My funding was coming from an American corporate sponsor. For this summer's work I was getting a stipend equal to the American minimum wage and a grant that had just covered my round-trip flight. It was going to be tight, but if I worked hard, and could get Jonnie through the summer, some good might come out of this for both of us.

"Okay, Jonnie-anna, here's my tent, my little home-away-from-home for the next three months. That one next to it must be Sondra's and that's where you'll be staying." I parked the Passnobile beside the third of four large, white canvas wall tents with front awnings, set on wooden platforms. Jonnie, obviously exhausted, blinked several times, fumbled for her packages and followed me into my tent. The ceiling was high enough for standing in the middle. On the left side was my cot and across the back ran a narrow desk with a power strip and communications plug-ins where I intended to keep my laptop computer and printer and do my paperwork. I dumped my gear on the bed then turned Jonnie around and led her over to the next tent where I could see Sondra was waiting.

"Hi, guys. Everything go okay in Mellankos?"

"Yeah. No problems." I peeked inside Sondra's tent. A narrow cot now stood against the right side. A thin mattress still high at its ends from being rolled up and folded bedding lay on its wire-mesh top. "Looks like they found you a bed, Jonnie," I said.

"Ah-huh." Jonnie set her packages on Sondra's bed and began making up her own. Since there really wasn't room for three people to work in the middle of the tent, I went back to the car and finished unloading. By the time I had everything set on the front part of my platform, Jonnie had gotten her mattress straightened and the sheets and blanket laid out and tucked in. I watched as she shifted her gear from Sondra's bed to a place under hers. She paused when she reached the fancy *kabusha* and, holding it in her hands, sat down on her own bed. She studied it for over a minute. Finally she looked up at me. "Jim, why do you do these things for me? How can you afford this?"

I shrugged. "I don't know," I answered honestly. "My mother and sisters gave me some spending money before I left. It's not a lot, but there was enough for today. I'd like to think they would approve of my using the money for you."

"Jim," Sondra put in. "You have to be the most hopeless romantic and nice guy I have yet met."

Jonnie: "Where do I wash up?" I asked Jim after I had refolded the floral *kabusha* and put it in the bottom of my suitcase.

"Washrooms—men's and women's—are to the left at the end of the tent row. They even have showers. Not too bad. You all set then?" I nodded, and Jim waved to Sondra and myself and returned to his own tent.

I got out my new towel, toothbrush and other washing up stuff. "Do I need any passbook, or anything like that?"

"No." Sondra smiled. "No one will check you in the bathroom."

I hurried down to the lavatories and entered the women's side. Although it was still light out, I knew if I did not get ready for bed now, I would fall asleep first. I brushed my teeth and washed my face as quickly as I could. I was finishing—looking in a mirror, examining my nose—when the door slammed and a young woman in a white tee-shirt and tight, black pants strolled in. I watched her in the mirror as she dropped a pink and green toilet kit on the shelf above one of the other sinks, glanced at me, stopped and turned around. "Who are you, and what are you doing here?" she demanded.

She was obviously one of my own people and not American. I slowly turned around, gathering up my toiletries as I did. "I'm Jonnie," I said. "Who are you?"

The woman could not have been much older than myself, for her skin and blond hair looked as young as my own. She smelled of perfume and cigarettes. "I'm Ilona," she said. "What are you doing here?"

"I work here. I'm going to be Jim Gailey's assistant."

Ilona snorted. "You're the little pickpocket I just heard about. Well, welcome to Castelschtop, but stay out of my tent, you understand?"

I must have looked the same as our pastor's dog did the day he accidently ran into the Madam Tredinstol's geese. "I do not do that anymore." I finally answered. "What is your training for the job you have here?"

"I'm Bob Covert's secretary."

"Yes. I see." I nodded. "Please excuse me. I'm very tired and would like to get to sleep."

"Be my guest," Ilona replied, "but if I have anything missing, I'm heading straight for your baggage to look for it," and she stepped well back to let me get by her.

Chapter 9

Jim: I heard Jonnie when she returned from the bathrooms, and Sondra heading there herself.

"Well," I finally told myself. "I guess she's all set. Time to get busy." I still had to finish all the data entry I originally had planned to do in the afternoon. I resumed typing and struggled for another ten minutes before knowing that it was useless. I was entering and reentering and correcting and saving the same notes over and over. I scrolled to the top, checked to make sure that I had at least gotten the earlier entries in correctly and quit. "Jonnie," I moaned. "It isn't your fault. I'm tired too." I retrieved my toothbrush then noticed the rose I had bought from the maimed boy in Mellankos lying on my bed. I lifted it and sniffed it, smiling at its scent, then set it down and headed for the lavatories myself.

When I opened my eyes the next morning, the first thing I saw was Jonnie, seated in my chair, her cloak covering her thin shoulders and half hiding the slip she must have slept in. "Hello," I managed.

"Hello," she answered back. "Do I start work today?"

I groaned and propped myself up on one elbow. "I guess so. Maybe, if I teach you, you can do some of my data entry on the computer." I shivered. It was colder here than it had been in Noviastad, and even there I had been glad to wear my cloak in the evenings.

"I would be happy to learn to do that," Jonnie answered. "But first, I must get dressed so that I will look respectable." Suddenly she was angry. "Whom did you talk to last night? The whole camp already knows I was a pickpocket! Now no one will ever respect or trust me."

I gaped in surprise. "I …I didn't talk or even see anyone after we got here last night. Except for using the john, I spent my whole time here in the tent."

"Then your professor-boss, Dr. Brothers, he must have said something."

"What happened?"

"I met that Ilona girl last night—the one who claims to be your American companion's secretary? She was using the facilities the same time I was. She knew who I was and that I'd been a pickpocket." Jonnie pouted. "She wasn't very nice to me."

Maybe I was not quite awake yet, or I was stupid. "How could she have found that out from either Tom or myself? Tom went to the motor pool, then, I'm sure, he went straight to his own quarters, which are on the other side of the big sorting tent out there. How could he even have seen Ilona—if that's her name—before she saw you?"

"I don't know. 'Bad news has a thousand reporters. Good news has only an editor.' My father used to say that." Jonnie shook her head sadly. "I'm sorry I accused you of being a reporter." She remained seated, cloak wrapped about her legs, as I sat up and tried to think about Jonnie's problem and about what I was going to wear. When she spoke again, her voice was quiet and almost shy. "Jim?"

"Yes, Jonnie?"

"Would you comb and braid my hair again—like you did for me yesterday?"

"Ah …Sure. Do you have your comb?"

She nodded, then got up and came over to my bed where she sat down cross-legged with her back toward me. She handed me her comb. I untied the shoelace and worked out the old braid with my fingers and began to comb. As I said before, her hair was thick, a dark brown mixed with deep red highlights and golden reflections. It still smelled slightly of the shampoo the hotel had provided with my room—a mixture of roses, honey and herbal sage. I took several deep breaths as I worked and savored the whole experience, even the braiding at the end.

After Jonnie had returned to Sondra's tent, I put on trousers and sandals and my fleece-lined windbreaker and visited the johns. When I got back, Jonnie was sitting on the edge of her tent platform beside Sondra. She was wearing one of her new work shirts, the brown *kabusha*, work pants and her new heavy leather boots. When she saw me, she immediately jumped to her feet and smiled. "I'm dressed. As soon as I have washed my face and eaten a breakfast, I'll be ready for whatever work you have for me."

"You've got a worker eager to work," Sondra laughed.

I grinned back. "I see, Jonnie-anna. Okay, let me get my work clothes on, and maybe the three of us can head over to the mess hall together. Make sure you have your meals voucher." I added. I pulled out clean jeans, a blue work shirt and my own boots and, of course, my dirk. After two weeks of wearing it constantly, I now felt undressed without it.

The mess hall/commons room was a tent big enough to hold a circus and its audience. Inside, a sea of tables and benches covered most of the free space. "How many people are working here?" Jonnie whispered to me when she saw all the tables.

I showed my meal voucher to the sleepy-eyed attendant and went through the turn-stile before answering. "I think there's a hundred-and-fifteen people here now, counting us. Another hundred or so will be coming up from Mellankos in a couple of days. Right now, most of the people here are the techies: students like myself, researchers, historians, archaeologists. The people coming up later will be the laborers—the diggers, the sievers—the people who do the real dirty work."

Jonnie took a tray from a pile and began going through the line, choosing a soup, several croissants and a packet of tea and a cup of hot water. I laughed. "Now I remember: true Starnovians never drink coffee—because that's what the Turks did."

Jonnie nodded and headed for one of the tables.

"Sondra is so nice. She gave me some of her shampoo and loaned me her extra pair of gloves," Jonnie told me as we ate. "Her tent's just like yours, 'cept she has pictures of her fiancé and her family set up next to her computer. His name is Tomas, and they are going to be married next year after she graduates. They met in school; her parents didn't pick him out or even meet him until after they had already decided to marry!"

"You find that strange? I guess maybe it is," Sondra laughed.

"How come you don't have any pictures of girlfriends?" Jonnie asked me.

I cleared my throat. "Well, first one has to have a girlfriend."

"Oh." Jonnie blushed and concentrated on her food.

The three of us were almost finished eating when a tall, dark-haired man with dark eyes and a trimmed mustache stopped by our table. "Gailey? Are you James Gailey?" he asked in clear, if strangely-accented English.

"Yes. I'm Jim." I turned and offered him my hand.

He took it happily, if a bit too firmly. "I am Dr. Emil Bayar. I am historian and librarian from Istanbul."

"Please join us." I gestured toward the other empty bench at our table. "How can I help you?"

Emil set down a hot cup of coffee and took the offered bench. "Good morning, Sondra."

"Good morning, Emil. We met yesterday, Jim."

Emil stirred his coffee. "Your Dr. Brothers tells me that you, Jim, are interested in the history of this special place. Excuse me." He faced Jonnie and offered her his hand. "I'm Emil. You are?"

Jonnie studied the offered hand for several seconds. "You are from Istanbul? You are Turkish?"

Emil laughed lightly and withdrew his hand. This time he spoke Jonnie's language. "You are Starnovian. I can tell. Please, I understand. You are part of a country with long memories. But that is why I come here, to bring you and your country more memories."

"This is Jonneanna Gilenhoff. She's my field assistant here," I explained.

Emil's eyebrows lifted. "That is a name rich in Starnovian history—a name you may be proud of."

"How are you bringing us more memories?" Jonnie asked.

"After the war of occupation, the Turks, my people, took many records back with them to Istanbul. Many were lost, but not all. I am here to find out what stories and records your people need. Then I will go back to our libraries where I will be heading up a UNESCO team that is trying to locate information about Castelschtop and that time. And, anything we find, we will be sharing with your scholars and historians here. That sound okay?"

"Yes." Jonnie now gave Emil a friendly smile.

We talked about Emil's work and how my own interests might fit in for several minutes, speaking in Starnovian so that Jonnie would not be left out. Then, with a wave for both of us, Emil picked up his empty cup and left.

"He seemed a nice man," Jonnie conceded as we picked up our own trays.

"Most people are pretty nice if you sit awhile and get to know them," Sondra pointed out.

"Mistress Sophie was nice to me." Jonnie whispered. "She knew why Nina died. I think that's why she talked Leo into letting me try to be a pickpocket. When she wasn't drinking or angry, she tried to help me. Even Master Leo was nice to me the one time I did succeed in getting a wallet. I hated taking wallets. Everything else was easy. But wallets …My hands would always start sweating, and I would start breathing really hard. Then I couldn't keep still or steady. Jim? I'm glad that's over."

"So am I." We were passing by occupied tables now. I noticed that almost all people were turning to stare at Jonnie as she passed, and I heard the word "pickpocket" being spoken twice as I went by. I took a deep breath. It sure looked like the whole camp did know now. I picked up my pace, eager to get out of there.

Chapter 10

"I'm heading up to the site as soon as I get washed up. See you guys up there?" Sondra asked when we got back to our tents.

"We'll be up in a little bit," I told her. "I have some data entry to finish first."

I washed up myself. When I got back to my tent, Jonnie was waiting for me. "You ready to start work?" I asked her.

"Yes, Jim." She stood herself up straight and nodded.

"Good. First things first. Come in here and sit in my chair. You need to learn the basics of my computer's operation. Have you ever worked a computer?"

She shook her head. "I have seen pictures; I have seen them in stores in Noviastad, but I have never operated one."

"Well, let's get started. You work hard, maybe people won't talk so much about your past."

Jonnie: Jim opened up his white portable computer. He had me push a button which caused the computer to turn itself on. Once it showed what he called its "desktop," I practiced opening and closing programs, creating documents and saving them. He showed me how I could create my own folder on the desktop and when I had opened and saved my first work processing document, he had me put it in my own folder. "You might want to practice writing. Maybe you could write to your family so they know where you are and that you are

67

safe," Jim suggested. "They might be impressed to see you can use a computer."

I nodded, but I knew I would not write my family. They were dead to me now. They had sold me and never expected to see me again. Why raise false hopes that I might be able to help them?

Next Jim explained how this computer was electronically linked to another computer in the headquarters tent and with a computer in the Antiquities Institute building down in Mellankos. These linkages allowed Jim to send messages to anyone else in camp, plus communicate with people all over the world. He opened a program which he said would put in a request so I would have my own electronic mail account so I, too, would be able to link to anyone else in the camp. I carefully filled in all the blanks on the screen he pointed to and, pushing the return key, sent the request off. "It usually takes a day for the people in Mellankos to process account requests. You should have your account approved and set up by tomorrow. Then I'll send you a message to test it? Sound good?"

I shrugged. Everything on the computer was in English and was so new and confusing that all I could think to say was "Okay." Still, when Jim announced that my lesson was over, I knew I was not afraid of the computer, and that I could reopen my own folder and reopen any of the files I had seen.

"So, was that so bad?" he asked.

"No—just all new. I learned some things," I told him.

"Tell me, Jonnie, do you know any English at all?"

"I know 'okay', 'hello' and 'alright'." I thought a moment. "I know 'whisky' and 'wine' and 'You got any beer?' I know 'yes' and 'no'. I also know what the English and Americans always said when they would meet me in the spirits garden."

"What was that?"

"Kid, do you fuck?"

Jim rolled his eyes and looked away. "Sorry I asked." Then he looked at me again and chuckled. "You're sure sophomoric. How about if I teach you some proper English?"

"Sounds good. Will it help me to work your computer?"

"Yes. And it will help you to help me when we're together with other Americans. Which alphabet do you normally use or know? Latin or Cyrillic?"

"I first learned the Latin. It's what our school taught, but I can read in the Cyrillic."

"Great. I'll use you for translating and converting since I've done almost all my work in just the Latin alphabet. Ready for a first lesson in English?"

"Sure."

Jim proceeded to identify twenty different things in English from his bed, his suitcases, and the table to the tent's canvas and the computer. Then he had me sit down at the computer, open up a word-processing document and type in each word five times. "This afternoon, I will give you twenty more words—if you remember all these first twenty. Do you think you can learn two hundred English words this week?"

"I'll try," I answered.

"Okay," he said. "Now I have to do some work on the computer myself for an hour or so. Do you think you can manage by yourself for that long? When I'm done, we can go up to the dig and find out what they want me to do today, and maybe you can help me there. Yes?"

"Yes," I answered.

"Good." Jim sat down in front of the computer, put on his glasses, opened a notebook which he propped up beside the screen and began to type. I watched him go clickity-click on the keys. I knew nothing about typing. I had to search for every letter in order to enter anything. That was another thing I would have to learn. I walked out of the tent and sat down on the platform to wait for Jim. Yesterday the doctor had said I should have glasses. At first I had not understood why. Everything I looked at had always seemed sharp, but now …I gazed up at the trees and the distant walls, suddenly aware of how soft and blurred everything distant appeared. Did these things look sharper to people with better eyesight, or with glasses? Should I ask Jim? I hated to give another expense to him—because I knew if I asked, he would buy me glasses and would never question the cost.

The morning sun was beginning to dry the dew off the top of the big tent in front of ours, shifting its color to a lighter tan. I liked the way the dark evergreens on the hillside beyond the tent set off its shape. This view gave me an idea. I reentered the tent and searched through a pile of folders and boxes under Jim's bed until I found what I remembered seeing.

"What are you lookin' for, Jonnie-anna?" Jim asked without taking his eyes off the computer screen.

"I found it," I told him. "I'll be right outside on our porch."

"Okay. I'll be done here soon."

It was a lined yellow tablet, and the pencil did not make dark lines, but both would have to do. Whistling softly to myself, I set to work. Soon the paper, memories and this view were my entire world. Before the war, I played the accordion. I started lessons once a week when I was five. By the time I was seven, I was good enough that the pastor of my church would sometimes ask me to play as part of a service. Everyone would always compliment me afterward. But it was the music that made me happy, made me want to play more and more. Box on my lap, straps on and sheet music on the stand in front of me, and I was off in my own world of melodies and sound. Sometimes I would play for hours and not even know I had been at it so long. The neighbors knew and commented, but I never noticed. That is the way I worked now at my drawing.

"Hi, girl. Who are you?"

"Oh, you surprised me," I turned to look up at the tall, clean-shaven young man with short, dark hair dressed in a blue-green jacket and loose khaki slacks standing less than a meter away.

"I'm sorry. I didn't realize how deep your concentration was." He sounded repentant, but I wondered if he had deliberately come up behind me in order to get the jump on me. This had to be the other American boy scholar. His accent was much stronger than Jim's. "May I see what you're doing?" He sat down on the platform next to me.

I shifted away from him a dozen centimeters. "It's not done, and it's not very good either," I told him.

He laughed lightly, showing white, even teeth. "Let me be the judge of that," he replied and gestured for me to give him the tablet. I reluctantly complied. He studied my work, shifting the tablet left and right and squinting at the view. "That's nice," he concluded. "You do nice work." Suddenly he stood up and called out "Hey, Ilona, come see what this girl's doing."

Ilona came into view. She made a face when she saw me, then turned to the American. "What is it you want?" she asked in an uninterested voice.

He laughed. "You know what I always want."

"Yeah, yeah. So, what's Jonnie here doing?"

"You know her already? She just drew this sketch of the main tent and the trees and the mound beyond. It looks nice, don't you think?"

Ilona lifted her dark glasses and gave the sketch a glance. "Not bad." She nodded to me. "You have more than one talent."

"Thank you," I managed, although I bit my tongue saying those words.

"Do you play the violin as well?"

"No. Why would I do that?" I responded, completely mystified.

"I thought maybe you are Gypsy."

"I am not Rom," I retorted.

"So, you are Jonnie?" the American interrupted. "I am Bob Covert, one of the few Americans here to help dig up this old ruin."

"Yes, I know. I am working with one of the others, Jim."

"That's right. This is Jim's tent, isn't it? You stayin' in here too?"

I wondered how I was supposed to interpret the word 'stayin'', but before I had to answer, Jim opened the tent flap and looked out. "Hey," he called out and greeted this Bob boy in English. They chatted happily for a minute. I understood only the words "tent" and my own name. Finally, Bob introduced Ilona. They chatted some more, then Bob waved to Jim, blew me a kiss and taking Ilona's hand, strolled off.

Jim watched them walk past the washrooms, then turn up toward the ruins. "So, I guess the whole camp does know about your past. Ilona and Bob heard about you from one of the team foremen who came up right before we got here. Bob said he doesn't know the guy's name."

I was remembering someone now: a man standing in the hallway outside of Dr. Brothers' office. That man? But I had closed the door when I went into the office! How could that man have heard unless he had been listening at the keyhole? "I think I know whom Bob is talking about." I described the man I had seen.

"Well," Jim allowed. "He sounds like a possibility. But why would he immediately tell everyone? And why was he so nosy in the first place?"

I shrugged. I could not understand either.

Chapter 11

Jim noticed the tablet. "What've you been doing?"

"Nothing," I answered. Nothing seemed worthwhile now—not if someone like Ilona was already working to get rid of me.

Jim touched my shoulder. "May I please see?" he asked. I handed him the tablet. He studied the sketch for some time, checking the view and comparing the results in the same way Bob had. "Have you ever worked in color?" he suddenly asked.

"A little," I admitted. Actually, working with watercolors was what I liked to do most of all.

"Then I may have another job for you. If I get hold of some paints and proper paper, I may have you make color drawings. Here, let me get something." Jim disappeared back into the tent only to reemerge a minute later holding what looked like a fist-sized rock. "Would you make a drawing of this for me—lifesize?"

Puzzled, I studied the rock, then set it down on the tent platform. Turning over to a new page, I began to draw, carefully trying to match my lines to the actual dimensions of the rock. "Like this?" I finally asked.

Jim nodded. "Like that. Okay. Bring the pad and let's go up to where the crews are working." He grabbed his fedora and a cloth sack stuffed with gear, and we set off in the same direction Bob and Ilona had gone. "You see, Jonnie," he explained. "Sometimes I think a drawing or a sketch can show a detail that even a sharp photo can't.

So, if you like to draw, I may have you make pictures of things we find. That could be another job for you. How's that sound?"

"Good. I'll try."

Ten meters beyond the central tent, an ancient wall rose to a height of more than seven meters—its thick, fitted white stones supporting the south side of the mound. A series of awnings shaded rectangular holes along its base. Each hole was marked off in square meter sections. Some of these holes went down half a meter or more, others were even deeper. A dozen men and two women were slowly cutting away the soil in several of the holes, carefully loading each trowelful of dirt into bins which others labeled and carried to the central tent. Everyone was working so slowly that it was hard to believe that anything was happening at all.

"Hi, Jim! Good morning, Jonnie!" I looked around and by one of the deeper holes spotted Dr. Tom standing with Dr. Bayar, Sondra and a stranger dressed in a tieless shirt and a rumpled suit. Jim waved and immediately headed over to join the four. I followed, holding the pad against my chest.

Dr. Tom gave me a salute. "So, has Jim given you anything to do yet?"

I nodded. "Yes. I am learning how to use his computer, and he wants me to make drawings of finds. Right?"

"Yup. She has talent. We'll keep her busy," Jim added.

"Good. We were just sorting out today's jobs with Sondra. Bob and Ilona were here, but he said they couldn't stay. I think they are going down to Mellankos for the morning. Sondra wants to stay with the plots we've already started. Jim, would you be willing to take the transit and start laying out the rest of the plots to the end of the south wall?"

"Sure. Okay. Any helpers?"

"Pavle has four who can help you. Dietel's one of them; he helped with setting up the first plots and knows how to use the transit."

"Sounds good." Jim gave Dr. Tom a thumbs up.

"Oh, excuse me. Jonnie, you haven't met Dr. Pavle Stiemenkovic yet, have you?" Dr. Brothers pointed toward the third man. "Pavle, This is Jonnie Gilenhoff, Jim's assistant for the summer. Jonnie, Dr.

Stiemenkovic is the representative of the Antiquities Institute and project chief."

"Pleased to meet you," I said and hoped my expression matched my words. What I really thought as I shook hands with this short, lean-faced man was: how can they be putting a Slav in charge of a project to uncover the history of my people's betrayal?

Jim led the way to the last hole where he gave me a tape measure. Three men and a woman in a plain *kabusha* and work clothes similar to my own joined us. Jim introduced me, and the man called Dietel set up the surveyor's transit and we all got to work—chalking out meter squares of ground so that the remaining space along the wall soon looked like a chess board. Using a black marker, Jim labeled stakes which he drove into points where chalklines crossed. I held the tape measure and later used the pad I thought I would be drawing on to take notes. By midday we had half the area remaining to the end of the wall set out in a grid.

After lunch, to my surprise, the work resumed. Our little team unrolled awnings and, setting them on poles, tied in ropes so that the whole area was under cover. The shade felt nice as the sky was clear and the sun had grown hot, but our respite did not last, for Jim wondered if we could get the entire grid done that day. "To be sure," Dietel replied, and the measuring and sighting resumed. By the end of the afternoon, I had a headache and was sure that I had never been more tired in my life, but we were done, and for a moment all six of us stood looking at the cross-hatchings spread out over a space as long as a football field.

"Good," was all Jim said, but then he shook each person's hand, including mine, and thanked us for getting this finished so that it would be ready for the digging crews.

The others left. I thought we were done as well, but Jim stayed to put the transit and its tripod back in their cases and deliver them to the main tent, then he returned to the plots and, taking a hand-held digital assistant device out of his sack, entered a series of notes, walking the area back and forth as he did until finally he sighed, turned the device off and joined me.

He gave my shoulders a squeeze. "Ready to eat?"

"Ouch. I'm sore. Yes, I'm ready." I answered, adding, "I'm tired."

Jim nodded. "I am too. But work had to get done. I had some good people today. Remember their names. If I get a chance, I want to ask for them again."

I took in his sweat-soaked shirt, sun-burned face and dirt-covered hands. "You worked hard yourself. Do all Americans work like this—right through the afternoon without even a break?"

Jim laughed. "No. Not all Americans are like that. Sometimes I can be lazy too, but …well, another American let us down today. I felt that I had to make up for him."

"Bob Covert?"

"Yup. I think that Tom was expecting him to do half that grid today."

"So our team did what two teams were expected to do?"

"That's what it looks like. You proud of yourself? You were the hardest worker out there."

I blushed at his praise. "I'm too weak to be much help."

"Don't downgrade yourself," he responded. "You're smart, and you pitch in. You can be anything in this world you want to be." I looked down at my new shirt, now all covered with sweat stains and dust, and felt the soreness in my feet. How could I be anything I wanted? I was just a Starnovian girl with no family. And what did I want to be?

Jim: We dropped our stuff off at the tent, washed up and headed to the mess hall. I had worked everyone on my team hard, including myself. Bob had blown it, as far as I was concerned—running off to Mellankos with his girlfriend—and I figured if we did not get that grid done, no one would respect any of the American students here.

I had Jonnie running the tape the whole day, deliberately working her hard because I had to know whether she really was a worker. If she was, I figured that it would not hurt for others to see that too.

Supper was beef gravy over noodles and lots of it. Despite her obvious exhaustion, Jonnie managed to eat her share. I think everyone did. Afterward, two men got out fiddles and another his accordion and we listened to an informal concert. Jonnie took quite an interest in the accordion music. I wondered if someone in her family had once played.

The music had ended, and people were leaving in twos and threes. A few were still lingering over cups of the highly-sweetened tea that is Starnovia's national drink, talking quietly or just sitting. Others were watching television on two sets placed near the kitchen. "Ready to go home to the tent?"

"Ah-huh." Jonnie raised her head from where it had been resting on her arms. "Oooh, all this smoke. I wish I could have a cigarette, one cigarette …"

We got up and headed out. "So why do they say 'Gilenhoff' is a name rich in Starnovian history?" I asked her playfully as we walked slowly through the twilight—Jonnie limping a little.

"The ancient kings were descended from the Grand Dukes of Gilendorf. I guess Gilenhoff was our kings' family name."

"You're right. I forgot about the connection of Starnovia with the old Grand Duchy. So, how'd you end up with a royal last name?"

Jonnie gave a tired shrug. "I don't know. It's my father's last name and his father's before that. It's been our name forever."

"Good. Well, time for all things tomorrow." I sat down on my tent platform and began wiping the dust off my boots.

"Yeah," Jonnie answered in a sad, wistful voice. "Time for all things." She slipped by me and stumbled into her tent. When I passed by two minutes later, I looked in and saw that she was sound asleep on her bed. I stepped up on the tent platform. Hearing me, Sondra turned away from her computer and gave me a wink. I grinned back, then together we eased off Jonnie's boots and pulled her comforter over her. Then I left to get ready for bed myself.

Chapter 12

I was the first awake the next morning. Jonnie remained dead to the world while I took a shower, dressed and put in half-an-hour on the computer—entering my account of what we had done yesterday. Then I switched over to the WEB and began looking for historical sources on the Grand Duchy of Gilendorf.

Moans and groans coming from the second tent put an end to my searching. A minute later Jonnie was standing by my tent's opening—blinking and disoriented. For a moment she looked totally confused as to whom she was or where. "Mmm. Did I fall asleep?"

"Yup, out like a light," I told her.

"Oh. Jim? Yeah, I'm still not awake." She disappeared. I was about to resume my searching when she reappeared, stretching and still groaning. "My nose hurts; my back hurts; my feet are killing me. You are a brutish taskmaster, Jim Gailey." I might have started worrying were it not for the upward curl to her lips. "These clothes are dirty, and I stink!" She clung to the front tent pole, swinging back-and-forth. "More work today, right?"

"Right," I answered. She nodded, then she was on her way, still mumbling.

She returned with still damp hair but in a better mood. "Oh, so much hot water!" she cried out as she again entered my tent. "It was like heaven. Mmm-hmm. Why didn't you tell me? I would have showered yesterday." She sat down on my bed and toweled her hair off again. "Do we have a clothesline?"

"No, but we can probably rig one. Where do you want it?"

"Maybe we run it between my tent and yours? I'll ask Sondra."

Sondra said no problem and even volunteered the rope. Soon Jonnie and I were hanging out the last of the clothes from yesterday that we had washed in a sink in the lavatories. When she was done, Jonnie reentered my tent and promptly sat down and rotated her back to me. "My hair's dry enough now. Are you ready?"

"Ready for what?" I asked.

"To comb and braid my hair."

"Is this to be a daily ritual?"

"If you're willing, maybe," she answered. I took her comb and started working out the knots her washing had put in.

After breakfast I reviewed her English words and gave her 25 more. She asked for 40, reminding me that I had promised her another 20 yesterday afternoon, but I stuck to 25. We walked down to the camp mailroom together where I picked up several letters from school and a postcard from my mother. Most of my writing to the States was going by E-mail, but it was still nicer to get letters. I wondered if Jonnie was planning to write her family, but she did not mention the idea, and I decided not to bring it up.

Getting a postcard from home reminded me of something I had yet to do. "Just a minute," I told Jonnie when we got back to the tent, and I got out my camera. "I need to get some pictures of you."

"Oh, no!" Jonnie protested with shielding hands. "Please, You don't want pictures of me now. I'm so ugly. My skin is burnt, and my nose is swollen."

"You're being silly. You look fine. Come on, stand by the front of the tent. No, not in the sun. I don't want you squinting. There. Good. Now smile as though you mean it."

Jonnie: I did smile eventually, and I did mean it. I just hoped that those pictures would never get back to Noviastad and would be the last. Little did I realize how many pictures there would be. Jim took pictures of me almost every day after that. Sometimes he got Bob or

Sondra to take pictures of the two of us together; sometimes he got others to take pictures of the whole group of us—Jim, Bob, Ilona, Sondra, Dr. Tom and me. Jim took pictures of me working, drawing, even sleeping. It was incredible how many pictures he took, but I never saw any of them. He used only film and shipped every roll back to America for processing. It made it easier, although it didn't help my curiosity.

The rest of that day we worked again on setting up the dig. Jim and Sondra took soil samples and put them in labeled plastic bags. I stood by, writing down the information on paper and later, on Jim's digital assistant after he showed me how he entered the data. We were in the shade most of the time, and it was not as hard work as the first day's had been. I saw Bob and Ilona on site. They were working near each other at the other end, digging with trowels along with other laborers. I smiled to myself when I saw what Dr. Tom had them doing, but I kept busy with my own work and did not seem to have any time for visiting.

I was sore at the end of that second day too, but not as tired. My boots were not bothering me as much, and I remembered to drink plenty of tea. This time we also took a proper break after lunch—a time I spent lying with my eyes closed and head resting against rolled-up awnings that had not yet been set up. I showered after supper and put on one of my dresses and felt almost whole again.

"You want to see whether your E-mail account's working yet?" Jim asked.

"Certainly," I answered and took my place in front of Jim's computer. I managed to log-on without his help and squeaked a little with pleasure when a window popped open that said in English "You have mail." The actual message was just a "test" note from Jim that said "Greetings from Jim to Jonnie. How are you doing? You do good work, and you are fun to be with. Jim."

"There you go," Jim called from his place on his own bed. "Your first E-mail."

"Do I get to answer the letter?" I asked.

"If you want to," he said. "Just hit the 'reply' button and it'll open a window for a return letter."

I did then paused. What should I say? It was so different putting words on a screen instead of speaking them. Finally I began to type, slowly picking out the letters.

"Dear Jim," I wrote. "Thank you for trusting me after I failed you. Thank you for saving my life. You are the bravest, most wonderful boy I have ever known. I will continue to earn the trust you have given me. We will have a wonderful summer. This is the world of my dreams. Thank you, Jonneanna Marie." I studied those words, knowing I was being all gushy and sentimental, but not caring. I hit the send key.

Later that night, lying in my bed and listening to Jim still typing next door, I considered the puzzle of our relationship. I was almost sharing living quarters with someone who really cared for me, yet not once had he tried to touch me or make love to me. What would I do if he did try to kiss me or make love to me? I felt so grateful for all the things that he had done for me, many of which were generous, sentimental acts—like his buying the flowered *kabusha*—yet did this mean he liked me too? "Jim, I love you," I whispered, and having acknowledged my own feelings, I rolled on my side and soon fell asleep.

In the morning the digging crews began arriving. By the next day the entire camp was packed with dirty, loudmouthed men and women, all grateful to have this chance to work and earn money. It was a busy time for Jim. He was constantly running errands for Dr. Tom, consulting with Dr. Bayar or supervising a part of the dig. The central tent was soon full of labeled plastic bins, each one of which held dirt samples from one square meter of the dig. I helped as best I could, but sometimes I spent time alone in Jim's tent. I discovered that Jim had a typing program on his computer, so, to keep busy, I practiced typing. I also began to read his English-to-Starnovian dictionary, picking out words in books and on papers and slowly translating them. He continued to give me new vocabulary, and, by the last day of that week, I did know the two hundred words I had promised to learn.

That day two of our army's Land Rovers rolled into camp followed by several fancy, black Rolls-Royce sedans. Men in dark suits or wearing army uniforms with braid on both sleeves got out. Dr. Stiemenkovic, wearing his usual rumpled suit but with a tie added, met the visitors and brought them up to the project.

Jim and I were at the east end of the dig, ignoring the visitors. He was checking the diggers' work, making sure that they were taking out the right amounts of soil and examining each trowelful for any artifacts. I was standing behind him carrying his camera and digital assistant and holding a drawing pad Dr. Tom had gotten for me at Jim's request. I was busily sketching the scene in ink—the bare, sweating backs, the grided landscape—and trying to show the contrast between the shaded dig and the bright, sun-lit areas beyond. Suddenly a stranger called out "Hold that." A camera strobe flashed. "Perfect! That was just perfect." I had my pad up in front of my face now, but it was too late.

"Excuse, Miss? You're a worker here too?" The photographer had her little notepad out.

I could not look up. "Yes," I managed.

"Good. Good, excellent. I am taking pictures for the Ministry of the Interior. Your name?"

"Jonneanna." How I wished I dared lie, but this was the Ministry of the Interior—the ministry that included the police.

She wrote. "Do you have a last name?"

I shook my head.

"Shy, aren't you. Well, that's all right." She turned to Jim. "And you, sir? Are you one of the Americans here helping us?"

"Yes. I'm Jim Gailey."

"Good. Well, thank you. Got to catch up to the others." The woman slipped her pad into a pocket of her vest and trotted after the group of dignitaries. I watched her catch up and speak briefly to a large, white-haired man who looked back at us. Then the whole group was coming back. Quickly the photographer began to choreograph a new scene.

"Looks like we're in for it, Jonnie," Jim whispered. He gave me a reassuring pat on my shoulder.

It did not help. I wished I could hide, run, be anywhere but standing next to Jim, Dr. Stiemenkovic, the white-haired man and two of the diggers while this photographer took half-a-dozen more pictures—everybody smiling, everyone happy to be working for this great cause, everyone eager to help Starnovia reclaim its past.

A week later the letter came. It was addressed simply to "Jonneanna Gilenhoff c/o archaeological dig, Castelschtop, Mellankos, Starnovia," but it found me anyway. Jim, his eyes filled with curiosity and excitement, brought it back from the mailroom and handed it to me.

If someone outside the camp knew I was here, it could only mean trouble. I took the letter and checked the postmark. Yes, I knew the handwriting as well. I turned my back on Jim, ripped the end off, tapped out the contents and, unfolding the single sheet of blue paper, began to read.

Chapter 13

Despite his curiosity, Jim did not ask or say anything. Instead, he returned to his own tent, leaving me alone to ponder the contents and inwardly moan. What was I to do? For one second I considered calling Jim or Sondra and sharing the letter's contents. A moment later, and I knew that I could never involve them. This was my problem. Jim had already done enough favors for me. But how was I to solve it?

I did not sleep well that night. All the next day the problem sickened my mind, so much so that even Ilona, who normally had time only for herself, asked whether I was feeling all right. At supper, Dr. Tom called Jim over and they talked, each looking my way several times. I felt my throat tighten. Did he know? If so, how?

When he rejoined me, Jim was holding a filled-out form. "Jonnie, how'd you like to go down to Mellankos with me tomorrow?"

"Okay, I guess."

"I'm going to take you to an eye doctor to get you fitted for glasses. Why didn't you tell me you were nearsighted?"

I shrugged. "I can see fine. I've never had glasses."

"That's not what the doctor wrote down when she examined you. Tom happened to notice the figures yesterday when he was filing someone else's physical. He wants you to get glasses, and he wants you to wear them—at least on the dig." He started putting his utensils on his tray. "Oh, and did you know that a picture showing us standing

84

with the Interior Minister made the government newspaper? Not good, aye?"

I shook my head. No, not good—but then I had already figured something like that had happened since I had gotten the letter. But I was going to be in Mellankos tomorrow! A seed of an idea was sprouting in my mind. Maybe, just maybe, that would help.

Jim: Ever since she had read that letter, Jonnie had been quiet and depressed. That night she seemed better, but sadder too. Passing by her tent, I noticed that she had taken out the flowered *kabusha* for the first time since we had come to camp. She was sitting on the edge of her bed, studying it, almost as if she were trying to memorize every printed color and every stitch of embroidery. When she finally put it away, it was with a sad sigh.

Taking my car, we drove down to Mellankos after breakfast. Before we left, Jonnie asked whether she could borrow my bookbag for the day and have an envelope and stamp. I gave her all these things without questions, but figured that somehow all of them had something to do with that mysterious letter that had found her here. I decided to be careful.

I took Jonnie to the only optometrist in Mellankos first, then to the market where she insisted she had to do some things alone. That was okay with me. I had my own plans. We met again at the car and ate lunch together at the Institute's cafeteria where Emil Bayar joined us.

"Why are you digging outside the fortress proper?" he asked half way through our sandwiches. "Do they think that King Stephen and his army willingly marched outside their walls and waited to be slaughtered? Now that I have seen and studied your fortress, I think I can find better answers."

"Where?" I asked.

"Back in Istanbul. I am flying home Monday. I will spend a week in my own libraries, then, if I do not find the answers I need, I will go to Vienna and check there as well."

"Okay," Jonnie said. "Good luck to you then."

"You, young lady, are a lion of a worker. The men see you coming, and they all get busy. Do you know why? Because none of them want to be seen working less than you. You are the hardest worker on the site."

Jonnie blushed and looked down. "I'm just trying to learn things. Besides, Jim here is a most demanding boss and teacher."

"That is true. Keep up the good work." Emil smiled and finished the rest of his coffee.

The next morning, the moment I had been waiting for but dreading arrived when Jonnie came running into my tent, the flowered *kabusha* clutched in her hands. "What did you do?" she pleaded, her words almost catching in her throat.

"I bought it for you again."

"Oh, Jim! Why do you do these things for me?" She sat down on my bed, lifted the *kabusha* up then let it drop on her knees.

"Why did you sell the *kabusha* back to the stall lady?"

"Oh …" Jonnie's hands shook for a moment, then she began wringing them. "I had to. I had to get some money. It was the only thing I had of value. I thought …"

"You could have asked me."

"No!" she was angry now, although the tears were starting to fall on the flowers. "You've already bought me the world."

"What'd you need the money for?" I demanded angrily. "Who'd you send the money to? Leo? Your parents? Who's blackmailing you?"

She shook her head, refusing to look at me. I grabbed both her arms and gripped them. "You must tell me!" She still just shook her head. I let go of her arms and took her head in my hands and lifted it, forcing Jonnie to look me in the eye. "I'm sorry," I told her. Why was it so easy for me to get angry? "I cannot help you if you will not tell me."

She was still crying, the tears rolling down her cheeks, one after the other. "It …it's Leo…and my family …" she managed.

I released her and sat back, my hands still burning from my brief touch with violence. "Leo? Was that who the letter was from?"

86

She shook her head. "No. The letter was from my father. He said that Leo saw my picture, wrote him and told him that I had run off. He's demanding that Father return the thousand fifteen *demkoi*. If my father doesn't pay, Leo promises that he would come to my village and kill my father—after he first kills my mother and brothers." She sniffled. "My father doesn't have that much of the money left, and if he returns what he still has, my family will starve. He says I must go back to Leo—that is my obligation to my family." She sighed. "I...I thought, maybe, if I sent Leo a little money, as much as I could, he might be willing to wait—or, at least, be willing to leave my family alone."

"The stall lady gave you eight *demkoi* back?"

Jonnie nodded. She was still rubbing her hands together, her gaze resting on some unseen place far beyond the tent. "I took the *kabusha* I stole back too," she added.

"Good. You think Leo would go to your parents' village and murder your entire family?"

Jonnie nodded. "Since the war, two families in my village have died in their sleep. Now their cousins and nephews are hunting those who did it, so they can kill the murderers' families. He'll kill you too, now that he knows you're still here and where you are."

"I know." I got up and walked to the door of the tent, hesitated, then stepped outside. "Oh, God," I whispered.

I felt a flutter of movement and Jonnie joined me. Shyly she took my hand and held it. "I'm sorry to be such a mess," she pleaded. "I didn't know what to do. I love that *kabusha* so much. It's the most beautiful one in the world, and...and you gave it to me. But it was all I had. I promised not to steal anything again. What else could I do?"

"You sent the *demkoi* to Leo?"

"Yes. I explained in a note that this was a first payment and that I would pay him the balance myself, and I asked him to please leave my family alone."

"Humph. So you sent him eight *demkoi*, and I gave him a hundred. That leaves nine hundred and five—equivalent to maybe three thousand American dollars. How did you think you were ever going to earn that much money?"

"I don't know." Her voice sounded small. "I guess I would have ended up doing whatever I had to do. I don't love my family. In fact, I don't care if I ever see them again, but they shouldn't have to die."

"Leo's the killer of children. He's the one who should be worried about his life."

"It doesn't seem to work that way, does it?"

I felt my anger returning, so hard that I could feel my stomach knotting. This was slavery, sexual slavery, enforced by a code of honor and a vendetta system as old as these mountains. Jonnie was locked in it. I was locked in it. "I think we need to talk to Tom Brothers about this."

"No! No! Please. If he knows, then Dr. Stiemenkovic will find out. The whole camp'll know, and no one will understand. They'll think I'm a whore as well as a pickpocket. Please, let me do what I have to do."

"No! I can't let you," I argued back. "You will not pay that man even one more unikos. You'll not sell your *kabusha* or your body, or steal, or do anything to raise money for that man. He took you from your family and the girls he has are slaves. No. Pay him nothing."

"But what about my family?" Jonnie pleaded.

"I will write this man and tell him that he's to leave your family alone. I will tell him if he has a problem, he is to come to me and talk to me."

"He'll kill you!"

"Not if I can help it." I had not the slightest idea how I was going to get either Jonnie or myself out of this mess, but I knew this was a matter I had to take care of myself. I had rescued Jonnie; I was responsible for her now. I would have to take the risk. But, oh, how I wished at that moment I was eight thousand miles away, back home in Massachusetts and safe in my own bed.

Chapter 14

Jonnie let go of my hand and stepped to the front of the platform where she turned around and stamped her foot. "Oooh. You are so stubborn! Are all you Americans like this?"

I laughed. "Blame my Scots-Irish ancestors. They never would take shit from anyone. Now, you give me that address for your former 'employer,' and let me write him a letter that might get him to back off. But, just in case, what did you do with that pistol you took the day I busted you out of his place?"

"The Beretta?"

"Was that what it was? Yeah."

"I still have it," Jonnie admitted.

"Tsk. We've some time. Get it out and let's take a look."

Jonnie gave me one last appealing look then led the way into her tent. She pulled her suitcase out and, fishing under her socks, retrieved the gun. "Thank you," I carefully told her as I took it. The Beretta was a 1927 model and had seen heavy use—the original brown and gray finish surviving only in patches. It was also still loaded. "Great! You've been sleeping here for three weeks with a loaded, deadly weapon under your bed?"

"I didn't know," Jonnie pleaded. "I've never used a gun in my life."

I scowled and removed the bullets from the clip, checked the chamber and put the empty clip back in the gun. I was figuring that this Leo guy wasn't about to come rushing up here until he had heard from Jonnie's family. We had at least a week of grace. Until then, the gun was going to be safer empty. "We will need a cleaning kit for this, and more ammunition."

"More ammunition?"

"Yes. I think I want to know how it handles, and maybe you need to learn how to shoot it too." I thought a moment. "Hmm. Where?"

"The camp guards have their own shooting range down on the other side of the kitchen. You know—we hear them on Saturdays practicing."

"You're right. I'll find out if we can use it too." I sighed and laid the Beretta on my bed. "Now, where shall we keep this that we both know where it is? And I need to write that letter."

We agreed that my suitcase was safer than Jonnie's and that way wouldn't involve Sondra. Then I sat down at my computer and quickly composed a two paragraph letter telling Buddy Leo that he was to butt out, leave Jonnie's family alone and leave Jonnie alone as well. If I found out that he was a threat to either party, I would make it my business to inform certain honest officials as to what kind of business he was in. I wrote the address that Jonnie dictated to me on an envelope, printed out the letter, initialed it, stamped it and dropped it in the mail on our way up to the dig.

Later I recalled Emil's skepticism concerning the location of the dig. The first chance I got, I asked Tom why the Institute had decided that the south wall was the best place to start.

Tradition, he replied. The Starnovians believed that King Stephen had massed his troops outside the inner walls in anticipation of the blowing of the horn and the arrival of help a short time later. Of course, tradition was all it was. No one would really know until the dig got down to the 1684 level.

"Emil does not seem to think it's a good choice," I noted.

"Emil may have a point," Tom agreed. "But neither you nor I are making those decisions." Tom lifted and resettled his Redsocks ballcap on his bald head. "We'll have the first squares down to the right level this week. If nothing shows up, I suspect that Pavle will be amiable to testing another site."

"It's still June. We still have two months to find something. Right?"

"Right," Tom agreed.

Jonnie: Once Jim mailed that letter, he acted like the problem was solved. I could not believe that anyone—Leo particularly—would give up just like that because an American wrote him and threatened him. But what else could I do?

The next evening Jim brought a box of bullets and a gun cleaning kit back to his tent. I was afraid he had spent more of his money, but he volunteered that he had done some favors, mostly involving computers, for a sergeant in the guards a while back and this was the payment he had taken.

Jim got the Beretta out and ran a tiny rag on the end of a rod through the barrel over and over until it came out white. He oiled all the moving parts and pulled the trigger once. Finally he seemed satisfied and put it away again. "Thinking about having to kill someone…You know, Jonnie, I never thought that would ever be part of my mindset. What a crazy world we live in! Well, what do you say that tomorrow we take the day off?"

"What? How can we? We both have jobs to do at the dig."

"Jonnie, except for that trip to Mellankos when we ordered your glasses, have either you or I had one day off since we got here?"

"No…"

"Okay. Your glasses are ready for pickup. Tom left a message on my computer that they're ready. So, what I propose we do is go down to Mellankos in the morning—leaving bright 'n early—then come back up here and take this gun down to the range and test it out. That should take an hour. We should be done before lunch. After lunch I want to head up into the upper ruins and take a look around."

"Huh? Why? What do you think's up there?" I asked.

"I don't know. That's why I want to check it out."

"Miss Gilenhoff? Yes, we have your new glasses. Just a moment, please." The service woman in the glasses store signaled for Jim and me to wait and walked to a back room, her high heels making little clicking noises on the bare floor. She soon returned with a pair of glasses in an ugly gray case. The glasses' brown frames were not pretty either but appeared sturdy. The service woman placed them on my nose and ears, making tiny pleased noises as she checked the fit. "They are just the right size. Can you see any difference?"

Actually, I couldn't at first, but when I looked out the window, the details and sharpness of the faraway world I was now seeing caused me to gasp. "Wow! I can even read that sign down the street." I shook my head. "I didn't think I was that blind." Then I laughed. When we left the store, I kept the glasses on so I could keep on seeing this new sharp world I lived in.

"We are a funny couple," I said to Jim as we headed back up to Castelschtop.

"How is that?"

"You have glasses, but you only need them for real close work. Now I have glasses, but I need them only for far away stuff. If we had children together, they would all have perfect vision!"

"Or vision so bad that they would not be able to see anything near or far without glasses," he answered back.

I pouted to keep from smiling. "You are such a black mop sometimes! All our children would have to be perfect."

"What God wills, is what we would have," he concluded.

That was not a statement I could have ever imagined Jim making. As far as I could tell, Jim did not even believe in a god—no more than I did. I studied his face. He was staring through the windshield ahead, his mouth drawn in a straight, hard line. Was this business with Leo worrying him? Or what? Suddenly I realized that I had been talking to him as if we were in a boy-girl, not a boss-assistant, relationship. I moaned. Stupid! What must he be thinking I was trying to do? "I'm sorry. Please, I never meant to suggest…"

"Suggest what?" Jim interrupted without taking his eyes off the road. His expression softened.

Now I felt totally stupid. "…suggest that we could ever be in a relationship other than…You know what I mean! You heard what I said!" I could feel my face getting hot.

Jim was starting to smile. "No, I don't know what you mean? What did you say?"

I curled up against the door. "I did not mean to suggest that we might someday be in a relationship where children might be a possibility."

Both of us were silent for the next kilometer or so. Finally Jim spoke. "I am sorry, Miss Gilenhoff, to hear that answer." That's all he said. The rest of the trip back to Castelschtop was made in double silence. He did not elaborate on his last remark, and I was too shocked and confused to know what to say.

Part IV: The Steltower

Chapter 15

Back in camp, Jim got out the Beretta and put it in his jacket pocket and the box of ammunition in another. He nodded to me, and we were on our way to the firing range.

The empty range consisted of little more than a steep-sided hole the size of my town hall's basement. The far end backed up against Castelschtop's mound. In front of this backstop several wood frames held tattered paper targets showing black silhouettes of men.

Jim poked around in the little wooden shack by the entrance to the range before emerging with two sets of hearing protectors and two new targets. I wordlessly put on the protectors he handed me while he hung the two new targets over nails, covering the old, shot-up ones. Rejoining me, he took out the pistol and began to load the clip with new bullets from the box. Inserting the clip back in the handle, he faced the hillside, rotated a lever on the left side of the barrel and sighted in on one of the targets. "All ready on the range?" he called out just loud enough for me to hear. "Commence fire," he added.

"Bam!" An empty shiny shell spun through the air to clink on the rocky ground; a tiny puff of smoke drifted away from the muzzle. With my glasses on I could just make out a tiny hole in the left-hand silhouette near its left shoulder. "Bam!" The gun spoke again, and another empty shell flipped up to blink on the gravel by Jim's feet. The target had a new hole closer to center of the chest. "It seems to handle all right," Jim said. "Want to give it a try?"

"I guess," I answered. Back in the spirits garden I had been so bold, flashing that gun around, pointing it at everyone as though I had known what I was doing. The gun had actually been loaded then! What would have happened if I had pulled the trigger? I held out my hands, knowing they were shaking as fast as my heart was pounding. "Here is the gun," Jim said. "Keep your finger outside the trigger guard for now."

I nodded. The metal grip felt warm where Jim had held it, the barrel warmer. I could not believe how heavy this little gun felt now. "Okay," he told me. "Step up to the line, point the gun down range. When you're ready to fire, release the safety, put your finger on the trigger, sight in on the target using the front and back sights and slowly squeeze the trigger. Be careful, the trigger is hard to pull at first, then gets easy. Understand?"

"No. I mean, yes. Yes, I understand," I answered. I lifted the gun, flipped the safety lever down and, still holding the gun with both hands, sighted in on the center of the right-hand silhouette. I squeezed, and the gun jumped in my hands. "Bam!"

I lowered the gun. "Did I shoot? Did it fire?" I asked. "Where did the bullet go?"

Jim came up beside me. "I think you hit someplace ten feet up the hill. You did not squeeze quite carefully enough. Try again?"

"It's awfully heavy."

"I know." He nodded sadly and backed away.

I took a deep breath. Why did I have to do this? I sighted in on the same target but lower this time. I squeezed, and the gun went off again, jerking my hands back the same way it had the first time.

"Good shot," Jim called.

I looked. This time the target had a hole about where a man's left ear would be. "I hit it? I actually hit it—didn't I?"

"Yes, Jonnie. Shoot again."

I fired the rest of the clip, pausing after each shot to check where the bullet had gone. The rest all hit the target somewhere, and two of the holes were in the chest area.

"Ready to reload?" Jim asked.

I shook my head. "No. I think I've done enough for today." I put on the safety, removed the empty clip all by myself and returned the gun, the clip and muffs to Jim.

Jim opened the top of the gun, checking, he said, to make sure no bullets were still in the chamber, then he stuck the clip back in and pocketed the gun.

"You learn anything?" he asked as he returned our muffs to the shed.

"Yes," I answered angrily. "I learned that I don't like guns."

"I don't either. Come on. Let's get this thing cleaned up and put away and go get lunch. Maybe..." Jim shook his head. "This whole thing's stupid. If I ever shoot a gun in anger, I'd probably end up just killing the wrong person or hurting someone I care for. Let's just forget it. Okay?"

I nodded. That sounded like the best idea to me.

We ate a quiet lunch apart from the others. As I picked at my food, I found myself glancing at Jim again and again, seeing a different boy than I had ever seen before, understanding that sharing this threat had added a new bond to our lives together. He had saved my life once already. Now he was voluntarily risking his own life again. Why? Did he really care for me? Or did he just feel sorry for me? He had gone along with that conversation about children, yet he kept a distance. He even carefully left my tent whenever I was changing or getting dressed. Was this just the way American men all acted? Maybe I was like his child, a stepdaughter perhaps? But what did I want? Did I want him to hold me or kiss me? Did I want to be a daughter or a girlfriend or...just an assistant? I stared down at my plate. Half a hard-boiled egg—its yellow eye surrounded by a white nested in a clump of noodles gone cold—stared back at me. What did being in love feel like? Nina had a boyfriend when she was just thirteen. They sat together in math and passed notes back and forth and ate lunch together. She told me that being in love made the stars and the moon brighter and bird songs louder. For the three months the relationship had lasted, she was the happiest I had ever seen her. If that was love, then this relationship could only be a disaster—since all I felt was sick in my stomach.

Jim: The target shooting changed everything. The hard cold metal in my hand, turning warmer with each shot, the perforations appearing in the black outlines of humans and the smell of the acid smoke had driven home the seriousness of the threat to both of us. Laying the Beretta back in my suitcase brought me the same kind of reaction that dropping an overdue book in the return slot at the library did—a feeling of only temporary relief with the consequences still to come. All during lunch, Jonnie said almost nothing, although I felt as if she were constantly staring at me. Did she hate me now for grabbing her arms the way I had the other day? Did she hate me for forcing myself into her business? Or did she hate me for demanding that she learn to handle and fire the Beretta? I kept wishing I had never, ever, involved myself with her. How much simpler my life would be now! But I also knew that I had no regrets about taking her away from that bar in Noviastad.

As we got up to take our trays back to the kitchen, the translation of an old Hebrew saying kept passing through my mind: "Whosoever saves one life, saves the world entire." Had I saved a life? Or had I just put two lives on the line instead of one?

"Oh, my. What a view up here!" Jonnie exclaimed when we reached the summit of the mound. "The tents must be fifteen meters below us. And look, I can see the gate and the road to Mellankos. Is that Mellankos way out there?"

"Looks that way," I answered. I took in a deep breath, glad to taste the fresh, dustless air that the grass and tree-covered summit were providing. I had only been up here once before and that was the first day I had been here—back at the end of May and a world ago, it seemed.

A few rebar posts with colored plastic streamers marked points the preliminary survey team had used to set up a grid for the entire site. The tops of shattered masonry walls criss-crossed the level summit, showing where walls and buildings once had stood. Pines grew in clumps and groves, pushing up against the few remaining structures that had not been either destroyed or quarried by locals. The entire mound had been certified as mine-free so, provided we watched where we put our feet and did not trip over a rock, it was and felt safe and peaceful.

"What's that tower over there?" Jonnie asked, pointing to the tallest surviving structure.

I started walking toward it, circling around a ten-foot tall crucifix made of iron and brass and framed by arborvitæ. "I think your people call it the 'Steltower'. It has its own legend, doesn't it?"

The structure was a round tower, close to twenty feet wide at its base and rising thirty feet above the summit of the mound, its walls built of cut and dressed stone. It had battlements and the only openings were narrow arrowloops, giving it a definite medieval appearance.

"Yes. The doorless one." Jonnie reached the tower and touched its surface before looking up at the overhanging crenulations. "I know the story. From this tower the horn player was supposed to sound the call for the attack. Only he left. It lost its doors because of the shame it felt for not being able to help save my country."

We began to circle the tower and, sure enough, we could not find any door, or evidence that it once might have had one. Back where we had started, Jonnie pulled her cloak closer to her body and sat down on a rock. "I like the way the sunlight is reflecting off the stones. I think I will paint a while."

"That's fine." I backed away and took a picture of her leaning back against the tower, sketchpad in hand—marking the first lines with pencil before she started painting. Then I sat down and just watched Jonnie for several minutes. She seemed happy now, softly whistling, away in her own private world. I felt content here as well, and wished that we could both feel that same peace down below or anywhere we went. I realized that I was afraid to go down to Mellankos again. The guards might be able to stop someone like Leo from getting in here, but who would provide any protection in Mellankos?

My thoughts returned to where we were. This tower was weird. How did anyone ever get in it? I studied the top. It looked too far up there for a ladder. Below? I studied the ground. It was possible that this ground might be mostly fill. Maybe an entrance was buried under rubble. I made a mental note to talk to Tom and check the aerials the first chance I got.

When Jonnie had finished her painting, she laid the work on a rock to dry, weighing down its edges with pebbles. Then, turning to face a different direction, she began to work on a new painting. I got up and joined her in order to sneak a look at her first work. It showed the crucifix—set in a coffin-sized slab and surrounded by the arborvitæ—and me, seated on a wall. I was impressed. Jonnie had left large areas of white space that became the white stones. The perspective and sense of place were perfect—a splash of blue for sky adding just enough color to balance the dark greens of the trees and the reds of the cross and my tartan shirt. In ten minutes she had produced a masterpiece while I struggled with automatic cameras and did not come up with results half as exciting.

"Hey, no peeking."

"Sorry," I said. "You're too late. I'm already admiring it. Jonnie, this is beautiful!"

"So, that one is for you, but what do you think of this? It's still not finished," she added.

The one on her pad showed the edge of the south wall and below it the sea of tents.

"Nice. I will stay away and let you finish."

"Maybe…Do you think anyone in camp might be willing to buy any of these?"

"I would think so. They are certainly good enough to frame and put on a wall."

"If I got two or three demkoi for each one, I could send some more money to Leo."

Her words were like a dark cloud stealing the sunlight. "I thought we agreed that Leo was not to get any more money?"

"That's what you said. But what happens to me once you go back to America? You may be safe in Massachusetts, but I'll still be here, and so will Leo. I do have to think about these things, don't I?"

"Yes," I sighed. "I guess you do. We both have to."

Chapter 16

"Hi, Jim. I thought this was your day off." Tom rotated in his chair in order to face me, his fingers digging out a fresh cigarette. "Here, sit. What can I do for you?"

I grabbed a stool and sat down. "Do you have those aerials of the site anywhere handy?"

"Well, I might. Or they might be back in Mellankos. I have two sets. I think one of them's up here." Tom began lifting papers on his desk.

His tent was twice the size of mine, or the one that Jonnie and Sondra were sharing, but he had still managed to fill it with boxes, papers, computer cables, filing cabinets and a host of other items, including a dead-looking pizza box. A bulletin board stood behind the back desk holding his laptop. Tacked-on memos covered half its surface along with bumper stickers telling the world to "BRAKE FOR MOOSE: IT COULD SAVE YOUR LIFE" and "VIRGINIA IS FOR LOVERS. I took all this in while drumming my legs with my fingers, trying to control my impatience.

"Ah, I'm sorry, Jim. I can't seem to find a set of them right now. Can it wait? I'll look again tomorrow, and if I can't find them, I'll bring up the set I have in Mellankos. I know where that one is."

"I guess I can wait."

"What are you interested in?" Tom tapped his cigarette and lit it.

I took a deep breath. "Just a wild idea—nothing that has to do directly with the dig."

"I figured that. Aerials won't show you anything we don't already know about the south wall." Tom coughed and cleared his throat, then drew on his cigarette.

The smoke was already getting too thick for me. I knew I was going to have to leave soon. "I was up on top today looking at the Steltower—you know, the structure on top that's still intact. Anyway, it has no way in. I was just wondering if the aerials might show something, give a clue as to where there might have been an entrance at one time."

Tom nodded. "Everything I've read and seen indicates that the top of Castelschtop is just a rabbit's warren of walls, passageways and buildings. Well, I'll do what I can. Say, how's your little assistant doing?"

"She's fine. She's learned how to use my computer and is doing some of my data entry for me. She knows enough English now that next time she's near by, I'd suggest you watch what you say." We both laughed. Tom gave me a wave, and I left.

Jonnie: I checked my E-mail. Tonight I had three messages: one from Jim, one from Dr. Bayar and one from Sondra. Jim and I had started exchanging notes the previous week, and now I got a message from him every day. He always wrote in English, which meant I had to translate it. He said that he was sending me E-mails so that I would get more practice with written English. That was true, but sometimes he said sweet things in his short messages that I never heard him say in Starnovian. He also told me that I had to reply to each of his messages in English. That was harder than translating his. At first it took me twenty minutes or more to put together a few sentences that looked as though they read correctly and had all the modifiers and endings correct, but now I could do it in ten minutes or less.

Dr. Bayar only sent me letters occasionally, and they were always in Starnovian. They were full of information on the dig and concerning the history of my country. I printed out each one he sent for Jim to read and always wrote him back right away to thank him.

This would be only Sondra's third E-mail to me. She was starting to write me too at Jim's suggestion so I would have even more English to read. I decided to tackle her message first.

"Dear Tentmate, (it read) I hope you had a nice day off with Jim. You work hard and are a good friend. Sondra."

I could actually read most of the words. "Nice" required a check in the dictionary. "Tentmate" was a new word for me but I figured it out myself, then checked to make sure. I began to write out a reply in long hand—first in Starnovian, then in English, carefully translating each sentence. When I thought I had it right, I clicked on the reply window and began typing in my new message to Sondra. Done, I sent it off and began to read the message from Dr. Bayar. It read:

"Dear Jonnie:

A colleague of mine located a cache of manuscripts taken from the warden's residence in Mellankos by the Turkish Army in 1684. They appear to include reports the warden received from King Stephen. Several of the documents are in an unknown cipher. I have contacted the military, and they have promised to loan us an expert to decode these. Ciphers were not very sophisticated back then, so we think that we will be able to read these eventually. Reports filled by the Grand Vizier Mustafa Koprulu indicate that the Turkish army was concerned about the massings of Starnovian irregulars to the south and west but after the capture of the fort, these troops drifted off without attacking ..."

The letter continued for another page, but, other than the coded letters, he had not found anything else new. I began typing a reply, working directly on the screen since I was writing in Starnovian. I told Dr. Bayar about getting glasses and about Jim's and my climb to the Steltower and how nice the view was.

Finally I turned to Jim's letter and began translating.

> "Dear Jonnie-anna, I am sorry that I grabbed you to force the information about Leo out of you. I should not have done that. I hope we have a good day off tomorrow, and the view from the top of the mound is as beautiful as I remember it was in May. Your supervisor, Jim."

I knew what "supervisor" and "information" meant. "May" caused a pause, and "grabbed" required a dictionary check. Otherwise, I was able to get through the sentences without too much trouble. Why was Jim so upset about his holding my arms? He had not hurt me or even really frightened me. Well, today had been a good day off—most of it, anyway. I started writing my reply.

Done with my computer chores, I pushed back from the desk and stared at the moving möire pattern that presently replaced the desktop display, its colored lines gliding across the darkened screen and bouncing from side to side. It must be almost dark out, since the screen was the only light in the tent—which meant that it must be close to 10 o'clock and already bedtime. I knew I should turn the computer off, get up and wash up. Still, I lingered, the dancing screen a soothing guide for my eyes.

A sound like fingers brushing a curtain startled me. I spun around and stared at the face and shoulder of a strange man just poking around the doorway flaps of the tent. Our eyes met—and he was gone. I heard a boot hit the boards of the tent's platform once, then silence.

"Oh, Lord of Thieves! Who was that?" I dashed out to the roadway, dropping my glasses back in place from their perch above my forehead, and scanned left and right. I caught one glimpse of someone tall disappearing between vehicles by the main tent.

"Hi, Jonnie? You're still up?"

I jumped. Jim was just coming out of Bob and Ilona's tent.

"Where have you been?" I cried.

"Visiting with Bob and Ilona a couple of minutes. Ilona caught me on my way back here. Said she wanted to talk about the dig." He led the way into his tent. "Can't figure out why now was so important. Neither she nor Bob had anything to ask that couldn't have waited until tomorrow. God, I'm beat. Saw Tom though and asked him about the aerial photos of the site. He said he'd have a set for me tomorrow. What are you lookin' so worked up about?"

I had to catch my breath. "That man, a man, was just in here!"

"What? Did I see him?"

"I don't know. I was just sitting here, and this man pokes his head inside your tent. The moment he saw me, he ran off."

"Oh, shit." Jim sat down on his bed. "Any idea who it was?"

"Yes. I think he's the same man who was waiting in the hallway in Mellankos when I had to go to see Dr. Tom about the cigarettes."

"The one we think might have spread the report about your being a pickpocket?"

I nodded. "Yes."

Jim: Here was a new problem layered on top of our problem with Leo's vendetta. What did this guy want, and why had he spread the report about Jonnie, and why was he now interested in my tent? He certainly had not come to visit. Jonnie and I exchanged looks

"No. Let's not load the gun. You have your *dirkosgay*. I don't think this man means to kill us."

"You're right." I agreed. "He has some other game plan. Although, God knows what it is."

"I'm getting ready for bed." Jonnie returned to her tent, grabbed her toilet articles and left for the johns. I walked out to the edge of my porch and watched her until she entered the restrooms building. Jeez! Were we safe anywhere? I looked back in my tent, taking in my computer, printer, my camera case and suitcases. If someone was a thief here, on site, what could I do? What could either of us do?

Chapter 17

Jonnie: Jim said nothing more that night. He said little the next morning either—not even as he combed my hair—an event usually full of chatter as we discussed what might happen that day. We ate in silence, our eyes roving the mess hall, looking for the tall, slope-shouldered man. Neither of us saw anyone that might be he.

Jim and I were back on the dig by 8 o'clock, working at the east end together. If we were somber, so was everyone else. The digging crews had been on-site for almost three weeks now, and no one had found any Seventeenth Century artifacts—not even as much as a button. The site itself had become a chessboard of dark holes and lighter tops—some plots having been dug down over a meter, others still waiting to be touched. I scurried from plot to plot, stepping on the ones that had not been dug out yet. As I took down notes and fetched equipment for Jim, Dr. Tom or Sondra or, sometimes, Bob, I could hear the men complaining about both the lack of results and the difficulty of the ground we were digging in.

Rocks were causing the most trouble. Once we got down half a meter, the fill was packed with sharp-edged rocks like nuts in a winter cake. Dr. Tom said that they were pieces of shattered limestone. He added that they had probably fallen here as a result of the Turkish cannonade that destroyed many of the old walls. His explanation made sense, but did not help the poor guys who were cutting their hands on the flakes.

I was passing by the east-most plot when one of the older men the others had nicknamed Pepe called to me. "Hey, Jonnie. Is there a canteen up there?"

"Yes," I told him. "An old army one."

"Would you hand it down to me, please?"

Pepe was not the best of workers, but he knew many stories and played fiddle in the evenings. "Sure. Just a moment." His hole was over a meter deep. I set down my work bag, which contained my sketch pad and paints and Jim's digital assistant, and, picking up the canteen, lowered myself into the hole. "Here you go."

"Thanks, Jonnie. You're a real sweetie." Pepe got up from where he had been kneeling and took a drink. I had one leg up—ready to climb out—when this gray ball the size of a large marble, caught my eye. I paused, then knelt for a closer look, pushing my glasses up onto my *kabusha*. "I think," I whispered. "I think I found something."

"What? What you sayin', huh?" Pepe screwed the cap on his canteen and glanced over. "That? That's just old pigeon shit." He turned away.

The heads on the old bullets for the Beretta were the same chalky, fuzzy gray as this ball. I studied it, tongue squeezed between my lips, thinking. In 1684, almost everyone was using a firearm. The soldiers had big, heavy guns they called muskets that required a lighted match to operate. Those muskets fired lead balls ten, eleven, even twelve millimeters in diameter. That's what this ball looked like.

At that moment, Jake, the principal site photographer, entered our area. "Jake, Jake!" I called. "Come here. Do you have a meter stick? I think I found something."

"What? What is it? Have you moved it?" Jake joined me in five seconds. Jim, hearing my voice, hastened over.

"No! I haven't even touched it. I think it's a musket ball." I could feel my fingers shaking.

Jake's eyes lit up, and he and Jim exchanged looks. "Okay, let us down there. Hi, Pepe. How's it goin'?"

"Looked like pigeon shit to me," was Pepe's unhappy reply.

Jim and Jake knelt down beside me and studied the ball. "Looks good," Jim said. "Good work, Jonnie. Good spotting." He stood up, giving me a smile and a thumbs up approval. "You got enough room to work there, Jake?"

"Yeah. I'm fine." Jake set a meter stick that had been cut in half (so it really only measured 50 centimeters) beside the ball and began to set up his camera.

Jim turned to Pepe. "How's it goin', Pepe? How's it feel to have something finally show up in your own plot?"

"Yeah." Pepe nodded and grinned. "It's about time, 'cept Jonnie's the one that had to see it."

"Hey, someone get a bin for this plot," Jim called. "Jonnie, would you make a sketch of where this ball is relative to this site and the others next to it?"

"Sure." I climbed out, retrieved my bag and pad and, sitting down on the top ground, began drawing.

"Hear we got something," Dr. Tom called to me. He walked out along the closest uncut plot.

"It's an old musket ball," I told him.

"Good. Jim, get the depth and its position on the grid."

"Jonnie's already sketching location, and Jake has several pictures," Jim answered.

"You guys are way ahead of me."

Dr. Stiemenkovic and Sondra joined Dr. Tom, both eager to hear the news. While Dr. Tom was explaining the find, Jim picked the ball up and held it high enough for everyone to see. "One musket ball— must weigh at least an ounce." Jim set the ball in a bin Jake was labeling.

"Jim," Dr. Tom called over. "Would you take over that hole yourself? I'm sending Sondra to join you. We need expert trowel diggers in there right now. Who's been working it?"

"Pepe," I answered.

"Okay. Tell Pepe to come out and come over here. We'll get him on something else for today."

"May I keep him?" Jim asked. "I want this to be a Starnovian find."

"You already have Jonnie. Well, okay, if you can use him." Dr. Tom waved, and he and Dr. Stiemenkovic moved over to a point where they could intercept Jake carrying the box with the musket ball in it.

"Hi, Sondra. You joining us?" Jim asked her as she arrived.

"Looks that way. Is there going to be room for more than two in this hole?"

"I don't know." The hole was a meter wide with perfectly-vertical walls. It connected to the next plot to the west so there was room for three people if they all worked on the side faces. "Tell you what. Pepe, I want you at this east end. Start to cut...Let's see, that's plot H-seven next to us. We need to bring it down to the same level as the ball was on. Sondra, you think you and I can lift rocks out the bottom here a little so we don't cut our knees?"

"I think I will get on top and haul the bucket up for you," Pepe suggested.

"Better idea. You're good, Pepe," Jim smiled.

"I wish the ladies would say that to me."

Jim and Sondra both laughed. "They will, Pepe; they will."

We ate a brief lunch and got back to work. I spent the afternoon sketching, taking notes and handing down water bottles. I also took photographs using Jim's camera. Jim and Sondra spoke English to each other while they worked—which totally baffled Pepe—but I found that if I listened, I could catch enough to follow what they were saying. By supper time, the three had cut the next plot to the north down to the same level as H8. Nothing new had shown up, and we were all thinking about quitting when I caught a gleam of yellow at the edge of the new dig. "What's by the wall?" I asked.

"Where? Which wall? I can't see it from down here," Sondra said.

Pepe joined me. "I can see it too. It's where you guys just cut and took out that stone."

"The one I just cut my thumb on?" Sondra asked.

"Yeah."

"It's slightly to the left," I added.

Jim and Sondra studied the spot we were pointing to, then Sondra took her trowel and began to cut around the place where the gleam was coming from. "Jonnie, call for Jake again, will you? I think we have a gold coin here. But there's something else too that might have been iron at one time. We need to record this and get a stabilization team in here pronto."

Everything had suddenly gotten so exciting, I hated to leave, but Jim and Sondra climbed out before I could even get my pad put away. "I'll get the yellow tape," Sondra volunteered.

"I'll find Tom," Jim added, and each headed in a different direction.

Pepe caught my eye. "A gold coin? Now that's likely to be worth something."

"I don't know. Will you stay to guard the site while I find Jake?"

"Sure, Miss Jonnie." Pepe grinned at me, then sat down at the edge of the pit so that his legs dangled into the hole.

By the time Jake and I got back to plots H7 and H8, a crowd was starting to gather. Men and women who had finished at other sites for the day were standing around in twos and threes watching Jim, Pepe and Sondra plant stakes and run yellow plastic around the perimeter. I could hear Dr. Tom in the hole talking excitedly to Dr. Stiemenkovic. "Please, can we get through?" I pleaded.

"Sure, Miss Jonnie," one of the women said, and she and others moved aside. "Now don't go stealing anything," added another. I glared in the direction of that voice but could not tell who had spoken.

"It's all right," Jake whispered to me. "Empty heads utter empty words."

"I wish," I replied.

"Jake," Dr. Stiemenkovic called. "Got another one for you, and she's a beauty. A gold *demkos* minted in 1672 and what looks like the head of a pike. We're waiting for guys with the plastic to stabilize the pikehead before we move anything." I stepped aside and settled in to watch, determined to remain until Jim left.

I had been standing by the pit watching Jake take pictures for several minutes when I heard my name and, looking up, noticed that Bob and Ilona had joined the crowd and were talking with Pepe who was pointing in my direction. Ilona caught my eye and in a voice loud enough that no one nearby could miss, remarked, "Well, it would figure a Gypsy would spot gold first thing."

I sucked in my breath. "You lying, dirty sow!" I hissed, and a wishful image of her standing with both hands pinned to a counter by knives flashed through my mind. What was this girl's game? Why was she spreading falsehoods?

Jim must have heard Ilona too, because he turned around and stared at her. He whispered something to Sondra and came over to join me. "It's almost six, you ready for supper?"

"What about here?"

"Tom and Pavle have this under control. We're not needed. Let's eat, then you and I can work on your report."

"My report?"

"Sure. You're the one that found everything."

"I…" I did want to get away from Ilona. "Okay. Let's go," I told Jim in English.

The biggest surprise of the day came when Jim and I entered the mess hall. Someone called out, "Here she is, our little gold-finder." Immediately, all the workers started standing up and clapping. "Hey, yea for Jonnie, from lead to gold!"

A thin-faced man old enough to be my father, reached out and grabbed my arm. "Tonight, you bring us luck. Now we know where to dig!"

Another man, his nearly toothless mouth all a-grin added, "The other guy said it was pigeon shit, but you knew it was gold. Good for you!" Such a whirlwind of goodwill! I felt so confused, I barely knew where to sit and what to eat first.

"A nice contrast to our neighbor's attitude," was Jim's first comment when he joined me. "They like you tonight because they think you've saved their jobs."

"How?"

"I heard a rumor when I was picking up our lunches today. Dietel told me that Pavle was talking with the ministry about laying most of the crew off until the survey team had found a new site."

113

"But this is just one little find—and it's way at the east end of the dig—right next to that huge rock fall."

"True. It doesn't look like there's much hope for the rest of that site. Maybe Pavle will want to move the rock fall."

"Maybe they'll listen to Dr. Bayar's ideas now."

Suddenly Jim leaned back and laughed. "You—even the day I met you—you've always had strong opinions."

I felt myself blushing. "I'm sorry. I still don't know much. I should be more modest."

"No, Jonnie. It's okay. You have problems; you try and solve them yourself. That's okay."

We spent the rest of that evening in the tent, writing up a report on the find for Dr. Stiemenkovic and Dr. Tom. It was hard work picking out the right words, but Jim helped, and when I finally finished a version he was happy with, he helped me translate it into English. We sent off a copy to Dr. Bayar. Then I had to do my daily vocabulary and E-mails and finally, tired to the core, I showered and got ready for bed. I was almost asleep when Sondra and I both heard voices in argument coming from Bob and Ilona's tent.

"Who…"

"Sh…" Sondra put a finger to her lips. I listened. The girl talking in Starnovian was certainly Ilona. But who was the man? Oh, how I wished I could be a spider in that tent right then! How I wished I could hear enough to understand why Ilona hated me enough to lie, and know whom she was meeting now.

Chapter 18

Jim: I was combing Jonnie's hair the next morning when she suddenly asked, "Why does Ilona tell everyone I'm Gypsy when I told her I wasn't?"

"I know you're not a Gypsy, but why would that be bad?" I asked back.

"No one trusts the Roma. They come, and they go. In my village they'll pave the streets with watered tar, then vanish before the rain. If it's a woman, we say 'watch out for your chickens', if it's a man, we say 'watch out for your daughters'. I know those sayings are just that—sayings, but many, many people believe them."

That was the answer I was afraid I would hear, although Jonnie sounded as if she was less prejudiced than most. "To answer your question…I don't know. She seems to have some kind of game plan that branding you with a Gypsy identity seems to be part of."

"Game plan? This is not a game."

"I'm sorry. A translation of an American expression. But I have an idea."

"What?"

"Would you be willing to work with Sondra today? She'd like that."

Jonnie pursed her lips in thought a moment before answering. "Okay. Yes, I would be willing, although I don't understand what that has to do with Ilona's calling me a Gypsy."

"Good," I said. "I mentioned the idea to Sondra several days ago. We can ask at breakfast. All right?"

Jonnie nodded and smiled. "All right."

The idea was fine with Sondra. In fact, she was so enthusiastic I felt a tinge of fear that she might try to steal Jonnie away from me. Still, I was glad to be away from Jonnie for a few hours because I wanted to talk with Tom privately. Jonnie was not the only person Ilona was affecting. Bob was not getting anything done at all, and this was making more work for both Sondra and myself.

Tom was already up at the dig, watching a backhoe begin removing some of the heavy blocks that were covering the base of the wall east of yesterday's find. A digging crew and a stabilization crew were in holes H7 and H8 working together to remove the remains of the pike and search for other items. Other crews were standing around with long crowbars and shovels, waiting to help the backhoe operator. "Hi, Jim. Pretty exciting today, aye?" Tom shook his head and started to walk away from the site in order, I thought, to get away from some of the noise. "It's been a pretty frustrating three weeks," he said once we got near the sorting tent. "I think even I was getting discouraged. Well, got to get down to Mellankos in a few minutes. What part of the project do you and Jonnie want to be involved with today?"

"Jonnie's working under Sondra today."

Tom stopped and faced me. "Oh? Something happen between you two?"

"No. I suggested it. I thought Jonnie might enjoy working with someone else for a day, and she might learn something."

"Fine. In fact, perfect." Tom resumed walking, heading toward his own tent. "I will admit that I've been both pleasantly surprised and pleased with the way Jonnie has worked out for you and the project. In fact…well…come on into my tent a moment. Can't hear or say a thing outside with all this noise. Good noise, though." He grinned and opening a flap, waved me in.

He took his seat and, excited and nervous, I grabbed a stool. This was turning out better than I had thought. I had been afraid I would not get any time with Tom at all.

Tom stretched and began searching his pockets. After he had his cigarette going, he leaned back and stared at the top of the tent before speaking. "Originally, the deal was that Jonnie was to get a place to sleep, medical care and food, and nothing else…"

Medical care? I thought. Where did that come in? Then I remembered: the Institute had covered her physical, her inoculations and her glasses.

"Jonnie has turned out to be a real worker—a lot more valuable than most of the people here we're paying money to. Pavle and I were talking about her last night. He asked what we were paying her." Tom looked down and shook his head. "I told him. He said, 'Starting tomorrow, I want you to add six *demkoi* per week to her wage sheet.'" Tom gave me a grin. "So, is that good news?"

"Good news? That's fantastic! Does Jonnie know yet? Man, where is Pavle coming up with that much money? Isn't that close to what the technicians are making?"

Tom shrugged. "I'm just the messenger in this affair—although, I will admit, a happy one. She doesn't know yet. I'll let you tell her when you get a chance. As to where is the money coming from? Pavle has his own resources. He said he'll cover the cost. And, as for Jonnie's status? That's what she is now: a technician. I noticed Pavle had several of her sketches on his desk while he and I were talking. He knows her work. He said that she's far more valuable than any ditch diggers."

For a moment I was speechless, blown away. This was the best news I had heard all summer. For a moment I forgot all the threats we were living with and even why I had wanted to talk to Tom.

Tom stood up, stubbing out his cigarette. "So, what were your plans without Jonnie today?"

"Ah…Work at the dig, I guess."

"Well, tell you what. Why don't you come with me down to Mellankos. We can go over the aerials together and maybe figure a way to get a sub-project going up on top. With most of the base site fizzling out and nothing new to do until we get those rocks cleared, Pavle and I have to start somewhere else if we want to keep these guys we have workin'. Something on top might be just the ticket."

"Ah…" Go to Mellankos? Did I dare? Leo might have my letter by now. But would he rush off to Mellankos to find me?

Tom must have sensed my hesitation. "I'll make sure someone gets the word to Jonnie before lunch, if that's your concern."

"Thanks. Yeah, sure. I'll go." Maybe I was being silly to worry. Heck, to work with Tom was why I was here. How could he justify giving me any credits if I never spent any time with him? "Do I need anything?"

"Bring your digital assistant, if you want to," Tom said.

"Jonnie has it."

"Well, then let's just go. I've got plenty of paper at the town office."

We saw Dietel, the transit man, as we were heading out, and Tom asked him to leave word with Jonnie. That done, we were on our way in one of the Institute's Land Rovers and once we cleared the gate, Tom started talking. "I'm going to tell you some things that are for your ears alone. You will tell no one else, not even Jonnie. Understand?"

I nodded. "Understand. Do you trust me that much?"

"If I can't trust you, I can't trust anyone." He paused. "We're thinking of sending Bob Covert home."

"What!?"

"He's put in only about five productive days since the dig started. He still doesn't have his own project even picked out, and he's taking time away from both Sondra and you. Both of you need time to do your own work. I don't want you to waste your summer cleaning up for someone else. There's another factor too…actually two others. One, he is setting a poor example for the digging crews. They may not love Americans, but they still think we're the most successful people in the world. May not be true, but when they see Bob hanging around with his girlfriend, it poisons the atmosphere for everyone. Second factor is the girlfriend. To put it bluntly, Ilona's useless. In fact, I think Bob might have worked out if it weren't for her. We don't need people like her on site."

"Excuse me. Tom, why are you telling me this? I mean, I agree. In fact, I was planning to ask you about Ilona, but why are you telling me all this stuff now?"

"Because, if the aerials look good, I may be putting you in charge of this topside dig, and we'll need to get someone new in here who'll work hard with the south wall crews."

"Oh?" I stared out through the windshield for over a minute. Finally I managed to get my mouth working again. "Me? Tom, I'm just nineteen. Who's going to respect me? Who's going to pay attention to anything I tell them?"

"I think you'll do all right. We're giving you Dietel, and Sondra will be up with you every other day. Look, nothing's final yet. I told Pavle I wanted Bob out on the next plane. Pavle wants to talk to him, maybe give him a week. If we send him home the first week in July, he'll have at least been here a month."

"Oh, gad…Tom, Ilona is the one who worries me. She spread the rumor that Jonnie was a thief. Now she's telling everyone that Jonnie's a Gypsy. She has something in it for Jonnie. I just wish I knew what it was."

"I've heard the rumors. I hadn't realized where they were coming from." Tom looked extremely unhappy.

"She apparently didn't start the rumors, but…" I described how Jonnie had seen a man in the Institute's hallway before talking with Tom, then added the incident where the man had looked in my tent. "…it seems a bit coincidental that he should show up the one night Bob and Ilona insisted I stop and visit in their tent." I added a description of Jonnie hearing Ilona arguing with a man in the other tent who wasn't Bob.

Tom didn't say anything for a mile or more. Finally he cleared his throat. "A-hem. Jim, You don't trust Ilona. I don't trust her either, but I don't know who would have been waiting outside my office at 4 o'clock that day Jonnie returned my cigarettes. Unless…No. No, I was talking to Aloyin Stepvenic, one of our crew chiefs, just before Jonnie came in, but he wouldn't have hung around."

"Is he tall, kind of slope-shouldered?" I asked.

"Hmm. Yeah, I guess you could describe him that way."

"Then that's who was hanging around."

Tom sucked in his breath. "Why would Aloyin be doing something like spread reports about Jonnie?"

"I have no idea," I answered.

I guess Tom did not either. He changed the subject after promising to keep his eyes and ears open. We talked about my history project and the information Emil Bayar was looking for and how I might tie this all together. Tom also told me they had someone ready to come from Germany to replace Bob if they sent Bob home.

Arriving at the Institute's building, Tom found an empty room with a cleared table near his office and together we laid out the aerial photographs of Castelschtop. Tom showed me how to use stereo viewers, and together we went over the matched sets again and again. "Okay, here's your Steltower." Tom pointed to the clearly-visible round structure. "It looks like a wall ran south here…"

"I see it."

"…then turned east toward where I think that crucifix stands."

"That's probably the same wall I was sitting on the other day when Jonnie did that painting of me I showed you."

"Much there?"

"No. The dressed outer stones stick up maybe two or three feet. The rubble interior is below the surface."

"Hmm." Tom stood back and took in the whole mosaic of photos. "You'll be in charge up there; you make your own decisions, but I would start by trying to locate the inner side of that wall. I know you're hot to find an entrance into the Steltower, and I agree there's got to be one somewhere. Should be one near where that wall attached to the tower. Well, that's where I'd start, anyway." He picked up the photo with the tower in it. "Looks like there's a way inside from the top. If worse comes to worse, we can always assemble some scaffolding and go in from there."

"Okay. We'll give that wall a try."

"It's not going to be easy. It's going to be all rubble and tree roots."

I sighed. "Yeah, I know."

I spent the rest of the day in the Institute's small library. Unfortunately, many of the works were in the Cyrillic alphabet— which prevented me from doing a straight read-and-translate. I had to constantly convert what I was seeing into the Latin alphabet first before translating. I was a pooped puppy by the time Tom found me and announced that he was ready to head back up to camp.

We were crossing the parking lot when a battered red Toyota truck caught my eye. It stopped, and a short, heavy-set man with thick mustache stepped out of the passenger side and returned my gaze. It was Leo.

For a moment I was not sure whether I should run, duck or scream. Then I realized he was looking as surprised as I felt, and both his hands were in the open. "Be with you in a minute," I told Tom and, putting my right hand in my jacket pocket and taking a deep breath, I walked directly toward the bar owner and pimp.

Chapter 19

Jonnie was sitting on the edge of my tent platform when I got back. The moment she spotted me, she was on her feet and running toward me. "You! You went to Mellankos? Were you crazy? What if Leo had already come up to look for you?" She grabbed my arms and glared at me. "He must have your letter. Why did you go to Mellankos? I have been so afraid all afternoon."

"Tom asked me to. We had work there to get done."

"But what if Leo had come…" The tears were starting to well up.

"He did. I saw and talked to him."

"Oh, Lord of our fathers!" Jonnie let go of me and spun around. I caught her by the shoulders. "You…saw…Leo in Mellankos?" She let me take her in my left arm and leaned against my shoulder. "I was so worried." Suddenly she shoved me away and stomped her foot in front of me. "What did you do? Did you kill him?"

"No."

"Oh. Now what are we to do? He will never, ever let go until your blood has cleansed his wound. I might as well…What am I going to do when you're dead?"

"Jonneanna Marie."

"What?"

"Calm down. Half the camp must be hearing us."

"I'm sorry." She lowered her head so far I found myself looking at the top of her *kabusha*. "I was worried sick. All this afternoon I have been trying not to cry, trying to work with Sondra, trying to be good, and all I could think was you in Mellankos, and Leo there and seeing you all white in the face and red in the chest."

"I'm sorry," I told her. "I did not know I was going until after you had left with Sondra. Come, sit down. I have much news—news I think you will like to hear."

Jonnie resumed her seat. "So what did you do to Leo?"

"I walked up to him and said 'Did you get my letter?' He just stared at me and nodded. I told him I was sorry I had used such strong words in my letter, but that I was just trying to protect you. Then he asked what I had done with you. I told him that you were working for me as my assistant. I told him that you write up my reports and take notes and were learning English. He thought about it and said; 'She's working for you? She was always a clever one—except at picking pockets.' Then he asked where she had gotten the eight *demkoi* that you sent him. I told him that you had earned it here, and that you would try to continue to send him more."

"What? How am I to earn any more money to send him?"

"Just wait. I'll explain. Anyway, he looked at me and he said 'You are a crazy American. No Starnovian would dare tell truth to a man who has sworn blood vengeance on him'. I answered 'It's easier to tell the truth. That way I don't have such a hard time remembering which version of the story I have told before.' He laughed then. But then he got angry. He held up his hand. I could see this big red scar on the back and in his palm. 'But what,' he shouted. 'Are you going to do about this? This is my blood, my pain crying for justice.' 'Okay,' I answered. 'In America, you sue. You take me to court and demand money for the mental and physical anguish you've suffered.' He stared at me as if I were nuts, then he laughed. 'You know, you are crazy American—but I like what you say. I have a cousin in New York. I'll write him and tell him to sue you,' and I answered, "That's fine. Tell your cousin I'll see him in court.'" I sat back and waited for Jonnie to speak.

She shook her head as if in a daze. "He's right. You are crazy. No wonder he did not kill you. We don't kill the crazy ones."

"Perhaps it helped that I had one hand on my dirk the whole time we talked…"

"So what happened after you said you'd see this cousin in court?"

"He asked me again whether you would be sending money, and I told him you would. He nodded and started to get back in the truck. I offered him my hand. He looked at it a moment, then he took it— very carefully. Then I said 'This is an evil world, and we are two men trying to do a little good.' He seemed to like that. He laughed again, and he left. Maybe he just laughed and left because he had no gun. Maybe he will still want to kill me later. Who knows." I shrugged.

"But where's this money coming from you're talking about?"

"Starting tomorrow, the Institute will be paying you," I answered, and I outlined what Tom had told me that morning.

When I finished, Jonnie could only shake her head over and over. "My paintings? Pavle has seen my paintings? He likes what I'm doing? Oh, Mistress Fortune, why am I so lucky?" She began crying. "Nina was so smart, and so pretty. Why'd she have to die, and I get to live? Why does the world do these things to us? Jim, I thought that my fate was to be the same as hers. Why am I still alive and safe with you?" Her sobs suddenly turned to chuckles. "And we spent all that time shooting that Beretta down on that range, and now there's no danger at all."

"We don't know that really, do we? You still have enemies in camp. But maybe the worst is over. Ready for supper?"

Jonnie stood up, wiping her eyes. "Yes. I'm okay now. I won't cry. I'll be serious and no one here will know I'm getting paid."

"Speaking of which, how much does your family need to live on—bare minimum?"

Jonnie paused. "Mother is earning two or three *demkoi* a week. If she or my father were earning six, they would have enough to live."

I got up myself. "I know you do not want to have anything to do with your family, but maybe, if you sent them some of what you are earning, your father might be willing to send some of your blood money back to Leo."

"Maybe I should send all of it to my mother and tell her to send money to Leo."

"You do what you think is best, but either you send Leo money, or get your family to. Either way, he needs to get something. I made him a promise—one that I think you need to keep for your sake when I'm gone."

We walked a while in silence and had almost reached the mess hall when Jonnie spoke. "Would it be okay if I kept one *demkos* a week for myself?"

I smiled. "So long as you promise it won't go for cigarettes."

"Oh, jeez!" She smacked me lightly on the arm. "No, it won't go for anything like that." She stared at her own fingers. "The first days here, I wanted a cigarette so much, all the time. It's not so strong a need now. That's one promise I know I'll keep."

We were halfway through eating when Jonnie sat up straight. "Oh, I have something to tell you too. Did you know that Sondra was originally Starnovian? Her parents were born here, and she was born here too, and she came to America when she was two years old."

I nodded. "I might have known something like that."

"Why didn't you tell me? But that's not all." Jonnie's voice dropped to a whisper. "She's Gypsy! When she told me, I said to her, 'I will not; I cannot believe you'. She asked me back, 'Is it because I do not fit the image of Gypsy you have in your mind?'" Jonnie studied her dessert, a kind of mystery pudding. "She was right. I did have an image. You know: dark hair, dark eyes, dark skin, hanging around horses, playing fiddle, driving by in a caravan. But then I thought about the real Gypsies I knew in my village. Some lived in houses, many were dark, but many were fair too. Sometimes I could look at a name and know; other times, not even the name gave a clue. Then I got thinking about the north Starnovians and the south Starnovians, the Palkan and the Slavs. We're all just people, aren't we?"

"Yeah, I try to see the world that way. Sometimes I succeed too. Of course, rednecks and weirdos are a different story."

"Do you have people fighting each other in America because of last names or skin color? I mean, I know you have people of African descent and you have people, Indians, who are descended from the people there before Columbus. Do they have a harder time?"

125

"Sometimes. Actually, many times." I thought about it, trying to figure out a better way to say it. "The world has two kinds of people: those we think we know, and those we don't. We fear, hate or avoid those we feel stranger to. Does that make sense?"

"Not really."

"Yeah, it doesn't to me either. I guess we both have to work on it some more."

Why was I so darn smart sometimes? I thought about all the things I had done and said that day as Jonnie checked her E-mail and began her nightly translations. Did I really know anything? Or was I just spouting out the balls of wisdom my father and mother had rolled in my direction time after time? Why was it so easy to talk to Jonnie? Did what I say just come out better or easier in Starnovian? And were we really free from Leo? He had not been as friendly toward me as I had indicated to Jonnie, but those words I said had been true. Who knew?

Chapter 20

Jonnie: We started our own dig on top of the mound the next morning. Jim had a crew of three plotters, including Dietel, to lay out the digging grid and twenty diggers to help. As soon as Dietel had the first squares marked with chalk and stakes, Jim ordered the diggers to start taking out small trees and lifting out and hauling away rubble. Every rock got a number and went into a special dump so that, as Jim explained, if someone wanted to rebuild the walls, the original stuff would be available, and masons would know which stones came from which section of the dig.

I loved the lighting by the tower, and I sketched and painted half the day. The rest of the time I took notes and acted as what Jim called his "gofer." In the afternoon, the gofer part seemed to consist mostly of carrying water and tea around to the diggers. It was hot up on the summit, and we had no awnings the way the crews down below did.

Only the top of the wall's outer exterior showed when we started. By the end of the next day we had cleared enough rubble and dirt to be able to see the finished backside of the stonework which Jim explained to the crew was our job to uncover. The wall had been over a meter thick and faced with the same kind of white, dressed stone as the south wall where the first dig was. The space between the two finished exteriors had been filled with loose rock and mortar.

The digging crews were less than a meter down when they discovered our first artifacts: broken pieces of crockery and small pieces of bone. Work stopped in that hole until a recovery team could join us and take the pieces away for evaluation. That night we felt good, particularly since the south wall crews were having a difficult time moving the rocks from the new dig area and no one had found anything new.

That night I had another surprise: When Jim joined Sondra and myself in our tent, he handed me a five *demkos* note. "What is that?" I asked. "I don't get paid yet, do I?"

"No. This is for your painting of the tents by the south wall that you did last week. Tom got it matted and framed in Mellankos, and Pavle had the Institute buy it for display in the lobby of their building."

I stared at the note. I could not remember seeing a five *demkos* note since before the war. "This is not real. Am I dreaming? Tell me I'm dreaming."

"You're dreaming. Check your mail and let's get to bed." Jim grinned at me and left to wash up.

Sondra and I were both in bed, and I think Sondra was almost asleep before I found enough courage to press on toward what I had been thinking about ever since that day when Jim went to Mellankos. "Sondra?"

"Hmm?"

I decided to start on safer ground. "I was thinking. Do you think it would be okay if I kept the five *demkos* note I just got? I mean, it's money I got for my artwork, not from my job here. And, if I sent a five *demkos* note to Leo, he might think I'm really making big money. Then he might get angry later if I sent him less. What do you think?"

"Sounds fine," Sondra mumbled.

"Sondra..." Now I had to get to the point.

"Huh?" Her voice was barely higher than a sleepy whisper.

"How do you...I mean..." It was so hard to say what I wanted to say. "What do you think Jim thinks about me?" Sondra rolled over so she was facing me. "I mean...Oh, I don't know how to say it!" I thumped my pillow in frustration. "How does he feel about me?"

"I guess he just thinks about you. You know: what are you doing today? What have you learned? How good a job you're doing. That sort of way?"

"That's all you think he sees me as then—his assistant?"

"I don't know. I guess that's what he tries to think of you as. Why?"

"It's all right. Never mind. Good night." I pulled my featherbed closer and bit my lips gently. After a while my fingers began to draw patterns on the wet surface of the pillow slip.

"Jonnie?"

"What? I'm trying to sleep," I answered.

"Are you crying?"

"I'm okay," I said, but I felt her fingers on my face, softly moving across my cheeks and around my eyes and dipping in the tears.

Then she was out of her bed and pulling me into her arms. "I'm sorry," she whispered as she rubbed my back and neck. "I never thought...I'm sure he never intended this. I know he's tried so hard to be good and fair to you, tried not to take advantage of you. You poor girl. I'm sorry." She touched my nose and lips, then withdrew, leaving me and my wet pillow alone together.

The wall we were digging out did run right up against the Steltower, and the fill went deep. By the first of July, our team was down two meters and beginning to find bits of red baked clay that Sondra said might be broken roof tiles. We also found an impression left by what might have been a leather boot and a piece of brass that Pavle identified as part of the mounting for a musketeer's gun rest. But we did not find any sign of an entrance to the tower.

The south wall crews began to have more luck. Under the rockfall, they dug up the skeletons of two horses and three humans with some equipment that indicated they might have been Starnovian soldiers.

Jim did not elude to Sondra's and my latest bedtime conversation, although he must have known. Sondra did not keep secrets about me from him. Publicly he treated me the same as he had ever since I had met him. Privately, he said less and when he did say things, I thought I detected a sadness and a concern. I wished I had never touched the subject of my own feelings for him. I began working harder than ever, trying to learn everything anyone would teach me. My English was still weak, but I started insisting that Dr. Tom and Sondra tell me some things in English every day so that I wasn't learning just from Jim.

A new student arrived from Germany, a fair-haired boy from Berlin who kept talking about someone named Heinrich Schliemann and how inspiring he found his work. His name was Jan Müller, and he never seemed to wear anything but khaki shorts and sandals, even among the sharpest rocks. All the workers thought him crazy, but harmless.

Which was more than they seemed to feel about Bob and Ilona—whom most people seemed to be ignoring. Bob was now spending most of his time in Dr. Tom's tent, or working on projects in Mellankos—leaving Ilona to sit alone by their tent. Some nights Bob was forced to stay in Mellankos. The first night that happened, Ilona slept alone. The next time it happened, Sondra and I could both hear enough to know she had company, and that company was a different man.

Jim's crew was working on enlarging the hole next to the tower one morning when I noticed Dr. Tom standing over by the crucifix, studying the tower. "Hi," I called. "When do we get to see what's inside?"

Dr. Tom shielded his eyes from the sun and looked my way. "Oh, hello, Jonnie? Didn't see you. You know, I think you've grown since I met you."

I shrugged. "I don't know. I guess, maybe a little bit." I looked down at my trouser bottoms, which no longer slopped over my boot tops.

Dr. Tom laughed good-naturedly. "Well, about time, right?"

"What are you looking at?"

"The tower. I'm thinking maybe we're going at this the wrong way. Instead of trying to find the entrance from the outside, maybe we should get inside first and see whether we can find a way out."

"But how, sir?"

"Ten to twelve meters' worth of scaffolding should do it, don't you think?"

"I guess. You're the boss."

"Well, I'm not so sure about that, but the scaffolding should be arriving today, and I'm going to have your Jim start setting it up tomorrow. Have you seen him?"

"Should be down in the hole."

"And what are you doing?"

"What does it look like?"

Dr. Tom eyed the surveyor's pole I was holding for Dietel and chuckled. "I guess I can tell. Carry-on."

All that day I watched as workers carried up the pieces of scaffolding. By the end of the day, they had assembled stacks of red-painted frames that seemed to cover all the unworked ground around the tower. The next morning, Dietel and Jim picked out a level site next to the tower just to the other side of the wall we had been digging out and had workers begin to put the pieces together. First they clipped two ends together with scissor-like side braces, then they placed heavy boards between the sides before starting on the next level. They had this new tower up to within three meters of the top when lunch time arrived, and everyone stopped. "Oh, Jim," I called up to him. "Must you stop now? Can we, will we get to see what's inside today?"

Jim laughed as he climbed down along with the other crew members who had been putting the pieces in place. "Hey, Jonnie-anna. Time enough. Look, it's gonna' rain and this steel gets slippery real fast. Let's not have someone fall off. Come on, let's go down to the mess hall to eat. We stay up here, we're both gonna' get wet."

"Phooey! I bet I can climb up into the tower right now from where you've stopped." I pointed to an arrow loop just above the last boards and above that to a break in the crenulations.

"Maybe someone with small feet like you can, but I know I can't. My boots wouldn't fit in that loop. Come on. We'll be in there soon enough. Don't forget the equipment." Jim began packing up the transit while I put my paints and notebooks away. He was right, the sky did look threatening, and a cool breeze was adding to the feel of rain. We seldom have storms during the summer, and I do not think it had rained more than twice since I came to Castelschtop, but what was coming looked as if it were going to be a ground-soaker. Sondra, Jim and I made sure Jim's hole was properly covered, then we all grabbed gear and headed off the mound just as the first flashes lighted the sky to the west.

The rain was coming down in sheets by the time we finished lunch—killing any possibility of a return to the dig that afternoon.

"What do you say we work in my tent?" Jim asked.

I watched the steadily falling water. "Yeah, I guess." I picked up my cloak and pulled it over my shoulders.

Jim stopped off in the sorting tent to tell someone where we'd be. "Go on ahead," he told me. "I'll join you in a minute."

Inside Jim's tent I listened to the thump and spatter of the drops on the canvas overhead, then sat down at the desk, started up Jim's computer and logged onto the mail system. Jim had not yet written his daily message to me, but Dr. Bayar had sent me a new one. I began to read.

"Jim, Jim!" I cried when he entered the tent. "We have a letter from Dr. Bayar. Look, read it. The experts have broken the cipher King Stephen used in his letters to the warden in Mellankos. And read what they say!"

Jim sat down and began reading. He got halfway through then started over, his lips moving as he translated. "So we're in the right place. King Stephen never did leave the walls."

"Yes, but can you believe what else he says the letters indicate?"

"That Stephen was planning to escape and not call in the troops waiting outside? That's a switch in history." Jim was shaking his head now, staring at the screen, reading and rereading the Starnovian words.

"Does that mean the horn player never was told to blow?"

"Maybe."

"Do we need to tell Dr. Tom and Dr. Stiemenkovic?"

"No, See here?" Jim scrolled to the top of the message and pointed to the header. "This is a shorter translation of what he already sent Tom and Pavle. I guess, if they decide to move more things up to the top, I won't have to worry about being in charge anymore."

I thought I heard a bitter-sweet tone in that last remark. "Won't it be good to be able to concentrate more on your own research?"

"Thanks, Jonnie. Yes, it will." He turned on the printer and hit the key combination that would order the computer to print out the document. "Rain or no rain, I think I need to go find Pavle or Tom, or whoever's up here on site."

"Okay. I will write back to Dr. Bayar," I told him. Jim put his cloak on over his jacket and, clutching the printout against his chest, left. I sat down in front of the computer again and began rereading the whole report. This time the information began to sink in. King Stephen sent three coded messages to the warden in Mellankos, who apparently was acting as a secret go-between to the Turks. Stephen did not believe his original plan was going to succeed. He wanted out and was trying to negotiate a way for him and his family to escape while leaving the remainder of the garrison to surrender on terms that would spare their lives.

Then I saw a sentence I had missed the first time that changed the last part of the old story completely: "I have ordered (King Stephen wrote) our horn player to leave with us. He has been quite resistant, insisting that enough people are waiting to come to our aid for the plan previously thought possible to succeed. I am afraid I must deal with him in another way." Stunned, I read that sentence again, and again. Our entire history—our whole sense of nationhood, of who was good and who was bad—for over three hundred years had been based on…a lie? Suddenly I felt alone and lost. Not even the tent could block the cold and dampness filling my arms and legs. No Slav had betrayed our king; our king had betrayed or tried to betray us? This could not be true! King Stephen died up there. His queen and his daughter died with him. The horn player did not blow!

I opened a reply to Dr. Bayar and began typing, angrily banging out a reply message. Only when I had hit the send key without even one check of what I had written, did I realize how much I was shaking.

Part V: The Horn Blower

Chapter 21

This was personal too! I bore a royal name. It had never made any difference in the way people treated me, but it was something to be proud of, a reason to hold up one's head in a village where status came from one's name or from the muzzle of a gun. These letters were saying that King Stephen, my king—the last king we ever had, maybe even an ancestor—betrayed his own people, or, at least, tried to. I got up and stumped around the tent, then lay down on Jim's bed and covered my eyes with my hands. Oh, what to think! I wished now that Jim would come back. I wished I knew what to do, wished I had someone to talk to! I pounded the mattress twice and moaned, then got up and once more read Dr. Bayar's letter.

This time it made more sense. He didn't say that King Stephen had actually escaped, just that he was trying to negotiate an escape. And it did give a different, but reasonable, explanation as to why the horn was never blown. I took a deep breath and began a new letter. When I finished it, I reread it twice, this time checking to see whether what I was saying made sense. Then, feeling much better, I sent it.

The rain, I realized, was no longer making any sounds on the tent. I closed the E-mail program and stepped out onto the porch. The clouds were starting to break up, and rays of actual sunshine were breaking through. As I glanced up to the summit of the mound, a new shaft of sunlight touched the tower and its scaffolding—a beacon beckoning me. "What are you telling me, tower? Is the answer inside you?" I whispered. I picked up my bag, checking to be sure the digital assistant and my paintbox and a sketchpad were inside. I added a flashlight then hesitated by the tent flap. Should I leave a note? I went back to the desk, activated the computer and opened a new document. Quickly I wrote in English: "Goed up to tower for few minutes. Jonnie."

Jim: What I had thought to be a quick trip to the main sorting tent and back took most of the rest of the afternoon, for if I had thought Emil's message was to be the surprise of the day, the news I was welcomed with when I entered the tent shoved it away. The south wall crew had made the biggest discovery of the summer right before lunch: the remains of dozens of soldiers, many wearing armor, many still surrounded by equipment. The crews on site had pulled some of the bigger items out before Pavle had arrived and ordered a complete mapping and on-site stabilization of the find. Now the preservation people were working busily to conserve the more fragile pieces that had been pulled out while others were working to map and photograph the pits.

I tried to get Pavle's attention. "Pavle, did you get the message from Dr. Bayar?"

"Haven't checked my E-mail all day," he answered. "Say, can you lend a hand to the technicians over there. We've got to get that armor photographed and in solution before it's nothing but rust. When it rains, it…Goodness, no pun intended. My diggers should never have moved anything!"

Emil's message could keep. This was crisis time. Feeling only a tinge of regret over leaving Jonnie alone in the tent, I dropped the printout on Pavle's worktable and went to join the preservation crew. Maybe, I told myself, I can get back to the tent in a couple of minutes to at least let Jonnie know what was happening.

It was past five before we had the easily-recoverable items stabilized and the site under control. I saw Tom only briefly. He had been in Mellankos all day and knew nothing about what had happened. I told him we had gotten rained off the mound, that I had been helping with the South Wall crews, and that I had to find Jonnie since I had left her alone in the tent. I forgot to say anything about the message from Emil.

Two of the guards, the chief of security, Sondra and Ilona were waiting outside Sondra's and Jonnie's tent. "Hi. What's happening?"

"Where's Jonnie Gilenhoff," the security chief, a short, red-faced guy named Goreski, asked me.

"I don't know. She isn't here?"

"Apparently not. We're looking for her."

"Why?"

"Ilona called us a half hour ago to say she saw Jonnie in the security part of the main tent where the artifacts are stored. We checked. The gold *demkos* is missing."

I could feel a sickness starting in my stomach. "Ilona claims she saw her? When?"

"I certainly did. You think I would confuse your little Gypsy for anyone else?" Ilona interrupted.

"She's not a Gypsy. You're lying," I shot back angrily.

"Stupid American. You believe anything your little pickpocket tells you?"

"Please. Please, may we look around, Mr. Gailey?" Goreski asked.

"Yeah. Go ahead." I said.

There was no sign of Jonnie. Her field bag was missing, but everything else was in its place—except, in her tent, Jonnie's suitcase was out a little farther than Jonnie usually kept it. Goreski began looking through things, being careful not to touch Sondra's stuff too much. He felt under Jonnie's pillow and ran his hands through her sheets and featherbed, then pulled out Jonnie's suitcase. He laid it on Jonnie's bed and opened it. Quickly he began taking out Jonnie's clothes and laying them beside the suitcase. "There will be a flowered *kabusha* in there that is hers," I interrupted, just as he lifted the gold *demkos* out of the suitcase.

"Shit," I hissed.

"Now," said Goreski. "The question again is: where is your Jonnie?"

"I don't know," was all I could answer.

I got to read the security chief's report in Tom's tent an hour later. Ilona claimed to have seen Jonnie in the artifacts security area between 2 and 2:30 PM that afternoon. She did not have a watch on at the time, but had checked the time when she had gotten back to her tent. She said that Jonnie was "acting suspicious, as if trying not to be seen." No one else had been in the area since everyone who would have normally been there was in the sorting tent or at the South Wall site.

"Jim," Tom placed a hand on my shoulder. "I know it's hard, but she was a trained pickpocket. It's not as if she came to us with any credentials. You and I both took her as an act of faith. Sometimes acts of faith fail. I'll admit that until now, she seems to have worked out remarkably well." He sighed. "Security says they've searched the entire camp, and no one has seen her."

"Perhaps she figured out she'd been found out and decided to take her chances by heading for Mellankos." Pavle suggested.

I shook my head. "It doesn't make sense. I mean, she was a little upset over Emil's message to her, but that wouldn't have turned her into a crook. Her whole future is based on her staying here. She has to earn money and she's doing that."

"If she needed money, that would be reason enough..."

"But how much would that coin have been worth? Maybe ten, fifteen *demkoi* on the black market? She would have earned a lot more than that working here over the course of the summer."

"Jim, we haven't said anything, and, in fact—outside Pavle, Officer Goreski and myself—no one else knows this, but we've been missing items almost daily for the entire summer. Some of the items have been pretty trivial—trowels, brushes—but we've lost some pretty expensive items too, including a Brunten compass, an angle calculator and two digital assistants."

"But what if Ilona was the person who took the *demkos* and put it in Jonnie's suitcase in order to frame her? I thought you guys were gonna' get rid of her! What's she still doing here, anyway?"

Pavle took a deep breath and looked away.

Tom turned red in the face and looked down. "Things have changed. We got Bob and Ilona working apart. That's what seemed important."

"So you're just going to convict Jonnie like that? Is it over? What if I say 'I trust her'? Doesn't it become my word against Ilona's?"

"Not quite," Pavle answered, "but if you can account for where Jonnie was between 1:30 and 3 PM, then it might be different..."

"...Jonnie needs an alibi, and a good one," Tom added. "But until she turns up, I don't see where that's going to come from."

By supper, it was evident that if Jonnie was anywhere, she was not in the camp. The security guys must have gone through every building and every vehicle in the entire place. I ate by myself, turning down even Sondra's company. The find that day had the South Wall crews celebrating, and the fiddles and accordion were once more entertaining a capacity crowd. By the time I had eaten half my dessert, I felt so depressed and sick, I just left.

I opened Sondra's tent flap, hoping to see Jonnie, or Sondra, and almost turned around and left. The sight of Jonnie's bed, with her suitcase lying open on it with her clothes still scattered everywhere, was almost more than I could bear. But then I realized that there was one thing I was not seeing: the flowered *kabusha*. "Jeez!" I began lifting her clothes—her underwear, her socks, her extra shirts, three dresses and one extra pair of trousers—everything else was there. Her two black *kabushas* were there as well. I thought a moment. Yes, she had been wearing the brown one today. So, the rest of the contents of the suitcase were still here. Where was the flowered *kabusha*? Was it in there when Goreski started going through the suitcase? Maybe—but I could not be sure. Who else would have seen it, known about it? Hands covering my face, fingers pressing against my forehead, I tried to think, tried to remember...Sondra? Yes, but no. Tom? No. Not a single person in the camp would have even known it existed besides Jonnie, Sondra and myself. Since I had rebought it from the vender, Jonnie had taken it out to look at several times, but I was sure she had never shown it to anyone, or even taken it out of the tent. Ilona? She had been in the tent today while Goreski was going through everything. No, I was the last one here. Unless she came back, she could not have taken it.

141

I slumped into Sondra's chair. I could not admit that Jonnie might have taken that coin—or anything else. Even if she had taken something, how could she have fenced it? She had been to Mellankos only twice since we came here—not like Ilona, who seemed to be going to Mellankos constantly there for a while. "No! Everything's all wrong! I don't believe it." I screamed.

"I don't believe it either?"

"Huh? Oh, hi, Sondra." I rotated her chair to face her and weakly waved.

"Ilona's clever, but now she's in a tight crack."

"What do you mean?"

"Where's Jonnie?" Sondra answered. "I think Ilona was hoping that Jonnie would be here so security would be catching her red-handed. If she had been, they'd have arrested her on the spot. You know what the police are like here. Innocent or guilty, they would have had a confession out of her by tomorrow morning."

"Yeah, I guess you're right. So what now?"

"You know another part of the problem?"

"No. What?"

"Tom's been sleeping with Ilona while Bob's been away in Mellankos."

"Shit! Are you sure?"

"Pretty sure. It certainly sounded like his voice in her tent the other night when Bob was stuck in Mellankos, and I happened to walk by there around 10 o'clock."

…and why he didn't send her packing the way he had promised, I added to myself.

"Speaking of our brave leaders…Pavle said you mentioned something about a message from Emil coming in today?"

"Oh. Yeah. Come on over to my tent, and I'll call it up." I crossed over to my place, Sondra followed me. I pressed a key to bring my computer out of sleep, and there was a message: "Goed up to tower for few minutes. Jonnie."

Chapter 22

Sondra and I stared at the words. Finally I managed, "I guess that tells us where she went."

"Would she have written a message in English?"

"Yes. She says a '...few minutes'? That must have been hours ago." I jumped to my feet and rushed out to the front of the platform. Sondra joined me, and together we stared up at the tower, just showing through the trees.

"Do you think she's still up there?" Sondra asked.

"I don't know. I don't even know why she would have gone back up there alone." I felt my shoulders slump. Did she know and flee? Did she not know? Could I find her up there and warn her? Is she still up there and hurt?

"What did Emil say in his message?" Sondra asked. "Maybe that's why she went up there."

I returned to the computer, opened up the E-mail program, found Emil's message and entered the print command. As I waited for the printer to start, I automatically checked my own mail. I had a new message from Emil. I noted the time: 15:23 hours. "Hmm." I opened the message.

"Jim: I got both of Jonnie's messages. She was quite upset when she sent the first one, but I am glad to see that she is calmer now. I'm sure that the revelations of King Stephen's secret correspondence were difficult to comprehend. Would you please tell her that I understand her reaction, and I am not angry or upset. Regards, Emil."

"Sondra, take a look at this message. It sounds to me like Jonnie flamed Emil, reconsidered and sent him a second message with an apology."

"What?" Sondra looked up from reading the information on King Stephen. "Please repeat."

I did, then added. "I left here around twenty after one. She was not upset at that time. If she reread Emil's first message—the one you have in your hand—got upset and flamed him, reread and reconsidered and then sent a second message, how much time would that have taken?"

"What's your point?"

"My point is, these messages might account for the time when Ilona said she saw Jonnie in the artifacts area."

"So, send a message to Emil and ask him to verify the times of the two messages. Every message has a time on it. We won't have to guess like Ilona. We'll know exactly when she sent the messages and even be able to confirm that it was from this computer."

"Sondra," I cried, "You're a genius." I began typing. "There, message sent. Now, do we look for Jonnie up on the mound, or do we share this new information with Tom and Pavle first?"

Sondra tapped her lips a moment. "It's almost dark and Jonnie's cloak is still here. If she's up there, she's starting to get cold."

"Let me call Pavle quickly first. I think I can trust him. At least, I don't think he's sleeping with Ilona."

"Who knows?"

I got out my cell phone and punched in Pavle's code. No answer. "Damn." I punched in Tom's code. Tom answered.

"Tom, it's Jim. Is Pavle there?"

"Yes. Just a moment."

"Hello? Jim? What do you need?"

"Got an answer for you as to where Jonnie was this afternoon."

"Oh?"

"She was in our tent corresponding with Emil Bayar via E-mail. We're waiting for Emil to confirm the times of her messages, but I'm willing to bet my summer's salary they cover the times when Ilona says she saw Jonnie in the artifacts area."

The other end of the line was silent a moment. "That's right. Any message would have date and time. I read the copy of the message Emil sent you. Strong stuff."

"Jonnie left a message for me on my computer saying that she was going back up on the mound and would be gone a couple of minutes. She still isn't back."

"You think her going up there is connected to Emil's information?"

"Could be."

"All right." I could hear Pavle sigh. "This certainly creates an awkward situation."

"I understand, Sir. Sondra and I are headed up to the mound to find Jonnie. Oh, and one other thing. Jonnie owns an expensive flowered *kabusha* that I bought her in Mellankos when we first got here. It is now missing from her suitcase. Would it be possible to have someone check Ilona's baggage to see if she now happens to have a royal blue *kabusha* with roses on it?"

There was another silence, then "Yes, I'll have someone check."

"Thank you." I disconnected.

Sondra touched my shoulder. "Jim?"

"What?"

"What's that sound?"

"Sounds like a tuba, or a French horn." Sondra's and my eyes met. "Where's a flashlight. Damn! My flashlight's missing."

"I'll get mine," Sondra volunteered. "And Jonnie's jacket and cloak too." She was out of the tent ahead of me.

Chapter 23

By the time the two of us were headed up the hill, the deep, vibrating blasts of the horn had brought dozens of other workers outside to stand staring up toward the mound. Sondra and I didn't wait for any of them. We trotted up the hill straight toward the Steltower, now glowing a dull pink in the midsummer twilight. We were still a hundred yards away when the sound stopped. "Hello," I heard Jonnie call down. "Who's coming?"

"Jonnie! It's Sondra and I. Where are you?"

"Up in the tower. I got up, but I can't get down. And I'm getting cold."

"How did you get up there?" Sondra asked as we approached the base of the scaffolding.

"I climbed up exactly the way I told Jim I could—using the arrow loop and the opening above it—but it's a lot harder to get down. I'm afraid to try it."

"Okay. We're coming up. Is the scaffolding dry?" I asked.

"Yes," Jonnie answered.

"Listen," I said to Sondra. "Let me start up first. Do you think you can attach some scaffolding ends to that rope there? We're going to need to get this thing higher tonight if we're to have any hope of getting her off." I grabbed two crosspieces and began climbing.

"Jonnie," Sondra called up. "How'd you make that sound?"

"I...I blew the horn."

"What horn?" Then I knew the answer to my own question and felt stupid. "Jonnie, you found the golden horn?"

"Yes. It was inside the tower, lying next to the body of the horn blower—what's left of him. I didn't want to disturb anything, but I'm so cold, and I couldn't get down."

I had to pause a moment to take everything in. "Tell us all about it later."

"I already wrote up a quick report on your digital assistant."

"Jonnie, you're incredible."

"No, just silly and impulsive." It sounded as though her teeth were chattering.

I reached the top boards of the scaffolding where I set the crosspieces down and began to haul up the two end pieces Sondra had tied to the rope and pulley system. I could see flashlights flickering among the trees and could hear other people coming.

"Hello. Need any help?"

"Is that you, Dietel?"

"Yes. We came when we heard that horn."

"Can you help Sondra get some more scaffolding sent up? And we need boards too."

"I'm coming up with Jonnie's jacket and cloak," Sondra called.

"So, Jonnie, you read Emil's news again and decided to check things out yourself?" I queried, as I untied the two end pieces, sent the rope back down and started setting the brackets in sockets one at a time.

"Yes. There is an opening on top that leads to a circular stair. The body is on the next level down."

"Anything left of him?"

"Not much. Some pieces that might be leather, the bigger bones."

"Any way out down below?"

"No, but there were two."

"Where?" I had both end pieces in place now and began to open the cross-braces and clip them in place.

"One is right below you, filled with rubble. We're going to have to move the scaffolding to dig down to it. The other goes out lower.

I think it comes out near the crucifix, but there's a big slab of rock blocking all but a crack. I couldn't get out. It was cold and damp down there. Scary."

"The entrance was on this side? We've been digging on the wrong side?"

"Here's Jonnie's stuff." Sondra said as she joined me. "Jonnie, if I toss your jacket up to you, do you think you can catch it?"

"I'll try," she answered hesitantly.

She caught the jacket on the second throw. By that time, the first boards had arrived. Sondra and I untied them and sent the rope back down. With the boards set in the next level, we were able to climb up another five feet and Sondra was able to throw up the cloak. I could see Jonnie peering over the edge less than three feet above me, her glasses reflecting off the light from the flashlight, her *kabusha* missing and her hair blowing in the breeze. "One more level, and we'll have you," I told her.

It took another half hour to haul up another section and get it set up. The last end section proved to be bent, and Sondra and I had to work and swear at it for several minutes before it finally clinked into place. As we maneuvered the last board into position, Jonnie climbed over the rampart and set her feet on the scaffolding. "Thank you," she said. "Where do you want the horn?"

"Oh, Jonnie." Without thinking, I hugged her. "Oh, Jonnie, you would not believe what a day this has been." Feeling her body against mine, I felt happy warmth then weak and a bit dizzy.

"Yes, I would," she answered as I let go of her and sat down. "I have been watching the guards out searching the camp for the last several hours. I knew something bad had happened. If I weren't so cold and hungry, I wouldn't have wanted to come down at all."

"I think..." Sondra interrupted. "I think we need to send for some plastic stabilization wrap so we can get the horn down without damaging it."

"You're right. Where is it?"

"Just right there. I set it on my *Kabusha* so it wouldn't get scratched." Jonnie said.

Sondra shone her flashlight over the top of the battlement. I managed to get back on my feet so I could look too and caught a glimmer of metal. "Is it real gold? Is it heavy?" I asked.

"It wasn't that heavy. I don't think it's real gold, at least, most of it isn't, 'cause I could lift it easily. It's just a bit bigger than an orchestra horn."

"I can see that. It's in beautiful condition. Are those jewels on parts of it?"

"Come on, Jonnie, let's get you down from here," Sondra suggested.

"No. Not until I'm sure that our horn is safe, and everyone knows the true story about what happened."

"Hey, Dietel? Is someone getting the stabilization stuff?" I shouted.

"They should be on their way," he answered.

"What is the true story?" Sondra asked. "You sound as if you found more than just a body and the horn."

Jonnie nodded. "He was shot—by my own people."

Chapter 24

"How do you know?"

"On the floor, in the middle of where his chest would have been when he fell, I saw a lead ball, like the one I found in June. It has a Latin stamp on it. I do not think the Turks would have stamped their bullets with the letters 'St'."

"No," I agreed. "I think you're right."

"I think he wanted to call in my people and was climbing up there to do so. I think King Stephen shot him, or had him shot, so he wouldn't blow the horn. I believe that he was our real hero, and I don't want anyone getting in there and messin' around with him until I can tell my people what happened." Jonnie was starting to cry. "They should take him out in a silver casket with our flag draped over it. And the horn should be on our flag, and our president should be here to salute him. Everyone should salute him. He died trying to do his duty. My people did not do our duty toward him."

Sondra and I each put an arm around Jonnie and held her. Neither of us said a word. I do not think we had any words to say.

The scaffolding began to creak and shift slightly, and I remembered that neither Sondra nor I had yet filled Jonnie in on what had happened below. "Who's joining us?" I called.

"It's Pavle. I understand that the sound we just heard was Jonnie blowing the horn of Starnovia." He stopped a level below us.

"Yes," Jonnie answered. "I'm sorry. I was cold and couldn't get down and couldn't think of any other way to let everyone know where I was."

"Well, the sound must have carried to Mellankos 'cause dozens of cars and trucks are headed this way. The phone has been ringing almost constantly for the last fifteen minutes. The Minister for Antiquities just called to ask whether it was true. I answered 'yes, it's true.' He's on his way from Noviastad." He turned to me. "Jim, Goreski searched Ilona's tent. We found the *kabusha* you described and one of the digital assistants that's been missing. The police are working on Ilona now." He smiled faintly. "I suspect she was not alone. Jonnie does not have to worry about the coin."

"Coin? What coin? What *kabusha* are you talking about?" Jonnie cried.

"Your flowered *kabusha*. Ilona stole it from your suitcase when she planted the gold *demkos* in there to frame you," I explained.

"My *kabusha*? Ilona stole it?" New, angry tears were forming.

"It's safe, and you'll have it back. Maybe you'll want to wear it for the Minister?" Pavle said.

"No, I will wear it for our president. He must come to salute the horn player who died trying to save our country. When he comes, I will wear it."

"Maybe, now that we have our horn again. Maybe he will come." Pavle finished climbing up to our level. "Now, I would like to see this horn that we have all dreamed of for over three hundred years."

Jonnie: Ilona confessed that night and implicated Aloyin Stepvenic, the crew chief I had seen in the hall at the Institute's building, as her accomplice. It turned out that he was her real boyfriend as well! Jim and a sheepish Dr. Tom explained that when those two learned I had been a pickpocket, they were afraid I might be a rival. Once they knew I wasn't stealing, they decided I would be a perfect scapegoat to pin their thefts on. The E-mail timings and the location of the stolen items in Ilona's tent proved that she had been lying.

The preservation people lowered the horn in a basket that night and took it to the main tent where they had it on display when the Minister of Antiquities arrived. Photographers took lots of pictures. I got included in a few. I mentioned to as many of the press people as would listen how important it would be to give the horn blower a proper burial. I was not sure it made much difference at the time.

The horn turned out to be made of silver covered with goldleaf and mounted with small rubies and a single sapphire sat just below the lip of the bell. The outer surface of the bell itself was covered with engravings showing hunting scenes. It was by far the most beautiful thing I had ever seen in my life—a sentiment that I think the entire camp agreed with.

Everyone was so excited the next day that almost no work got done at either dig. That night I climbed on the stage at the end of the mess hall, borrowed the accordion and played for the whole tent. At first it was exciting and fun, but then I thought about my village, and the memories of growing up made me cry. When I finished, the applause went on so long I had to play two more tunes before anyone would let me leave.

When Jim and I got back to my tent the next night, we discovered a new accordion all mounted in blue and yellow waiting for me. We never did find out who had bought it, or how he, she or they had gotten it up to Castelschtop so quickly, but I did not really care because it felt so wonderful to be able to play my own instrument again.

Over the next two weeks life returned to almost normal. The dig at the base of the south wall petered out and all the crews moved to the summit. A crew took the scaffolding down, moved it, set it back up and dug out the doorway. Then another crew removed the horn blower's body and went through the entire tower. Bob Covert took an early flight home, and the German boy took over his duties and projects.

I enjoyed those days. I worked on my English and wrote up reports with Jim every night. As my English skills improved, he told me stories about his growing up and about his family and friends back in America. I told him about my village and more about my family. We talked about many, many things, except…except neither of us talked about what was to happen the 28th of August when Jim would leave and return to America.

Dr. Bayar rejoined the dig the last week in July. He brought with him new maps of the site and new ideas as to where to dig and where to look. The first time he saw me, he jumped back in surprise, then he smiled. "Jonnie! I didn't recognize you. How much have you grown? Two, three centimeters?"

"Over three," I admitted.

"You are no longer the skinny girl I saw back in June. You look so grown up."

I nodded. "Jim bought me all new clothes last week."

"Just last week? He hadn't noticed before? The man's a fool if he has not seen what you have become. You are a beautiful, young lady now."

I did blush then, but he was right. I was no longer skin-and-bones, and I think I would have been lost in this camp filled with men without Sondra. She gave me American girl-style advice, and took me to Mellankos when I needed female things—helping me shop for new underclothes and even helped me pick out a silver necklace to wear which I bought with my own money.

I got paid once a week and each week I sent one *demkos* to my family and three *demkoi* to Leo. At first he acknowledged these payments with short, polite return notes, but after the publicity concerning the horn appeared in all the national newspapers and on our state television, his notes became demanding and nasty. He insisted that I send him five *demkoi* each week and that my family still return part of the money he had paid them. He wrote that if I did not do this, he would kill Jim, and he reminded me that he still had blood claim on Jim, so no court would convict him. He was right; our courts never convicted any man who claimed blood rights to someone. But what was I to do?

Part VI: The Burial

Chapter 25

This time I decided that I would not keep a secret and showed Jim the latest letter. He read it slowly, taking his time since Leo wrote in the Cyrillic alphabet. "Let's go to Pavle," he said.

Jim was no longer spending much time with Dr. Tom. While he had not said much, I think the idea of his boss sleeping with another student's mistress upset him a great deal. I, also, had lost a lot of my respect for Dr. Tom. Instead, both of us were mostly working with Dr. Stiemenkovic and Dr. Bayar, and Jim had built a close working relationship with the Turkish librarian.

It was nearly supper before we got to see Dr. Stiemenkovic. When Jim explained the story of how we had met and what my former owner was trying to do, Dr. Stiemenkovic became angry, his hands closing into fists again and again. Twice he got up and walked around the space behind his desk. When Jim finished, he looked at me. "Jonnie, all this is true?"

"Yes," I managed.

"Jonnie, our president knows about you. And I understand from conversations with the minister, he's very concerned about the 'golden girls' and what that is doing to our reputation as a country and a people." He sat back down, picked up a paper, put it down and sighed before continuing. "We need to attract foreign visitors who will bring money to help us recover from the war. But we don't need old men lusting for our children. We need Americans and Germans and others interested in history, not bare bottoms. Castelschtop is part of our president's plan to solve this. The dig is part of his plan. He wants to restore Castelschtop; he wants to build a museum here to house all the artifacts we have found and ones we have yet to find, but will. There has been a fortress here for a thousand years. I know we still have many things to find. Finding the horn, our horn, was the key. Now he has something big, something important, to show the world, something that will attract people from all over the world. No, this is not the Acropolis or Vatican City, but it is the navel of our nation.

"Do not worry about your Leo. Do not worry about your companions back in Noviastad. Now that he has an alternative, our president will be making changes. I do not know what all of them will be, but..." Dr. Stiemenkovic looked me straight in the eye. "He has read your report about the horn blower. Did you know that he was a boy, no more than fifteen or sixteen years old? Yes, he was a hero, an example for all of us—and one of our youth. Your report has gone to all the ministries. There will be changes and, yes, the president will be coming here to meet you and honor our dead hero."

Neither Jim nor I wrote to Leo again, nor did I send him any more money. Three days later we watched on state television as the president announced that any keeping of prostitutes younger than eighteen would be punishable by up to five years imprisonment and would include an immediate loss of liquor license. The police were already visiting the spirits gardens in Noviastad where they were checking all passbooks. Underage girls would be removed and either sent back to their homes, or be cared for. The speech went on and on, and I soon lost track of the details. "I think Leo's going to be out of business," Jim whispered to me.

"Was that what Dr. Stiemenkovic meant? Are we really free?"

Jim shrugged. "It doesn't sound like he's going to be in any position to collect any more money from either you or your parents."

"But that won't prevent Leo from claiming your blood," I exclaimed.

"No," Jim admitted. "It won't."

Jim: On August 1st a paving crew began working on the road between Mellankos and Castelschtop, and surveyors began to lay out the site for the building that would be the museum to house the artifacts. New workers began arriving: masons, artisans, restorers. They began to sort through the loose stones on top of the mound and two days later started rebuilding the wall that ran from the tower to the crucifix. They restored the excavated entry to the tower and installed a new red tile roof on top. Jonnie and I kept busy writing up descriptions for each floor of the tower so that visitors would be able to read something about the tower's history as they walked through. I wrote first in English, then Jonnie wrote in Starnovian. Jan Müller helped with the German and French, and Emil wrote a version in Turkish and Serbo-Croatian. By the time we had one notice ready in all the local and international languages, the printouts covered half a wall for each floor. We had to cut the text in half and redo all the translations again before we had everything down to a length that satisfied Pavle.

On August 8th, Pavle announced at dinner that on the 10th, his excellency, Mikail Vorostavos, President of the Republic of Starnovia, would be coming in person to Castelschtop to view the site and inspect the finds. He would also be attending a service for the internment of the horn player, a hero of which all of Starnovia could be proud. It was a set speech, read from a piece of paper, but Pavle's voice broke once anyway. When he finished, the whole place erupted in shouts of happiness. In the middle of all this noise I noticed that Jonnie was starting to cry. "Now what are you unhappy about?" I shouted.

"I'm not unhappy; I am so happy. Our president listened to me. We, all my people, will have one hero to share."

"Come here, Jonnie." I held out my arms. "You cry for everything, don't you?"

She nodded and nestled in my arms while the people nearest us looked away. "I try not to, but it happens anyway. All my family cries all the time. We're a sentimental people, I guess."

Tom joined us. "The president wants Jonnie to be part of the service. I have been told to make sure she has a proper outfit for the occasion."

"You?" I laughed. "Why don't you delegate that to Sondra."

"Maybe that would be better," Tom admitted.

"If I wash my trousers and press one of my shirts, would that be good enough?" Jonnie asked with a hint of mischief. "I can even clean, wax and polish my boots."

Tom rolled his eyes. "I think they're wanting something more in the way of a dress."

The next day Tom, Sondra and Jonnie drove to Mellankos over the newly paved road. They were gone most of the day leaving me behind to worry, but my nail-chewing was ill-founded, for Jonnie returned safely and that night she and Sondra showed me this full-sleeved, white blouse covered with gold embroidery, a white apron and a dark green skirt with three petticoats. Embroidered roses covered the six inches above the skirt's hem, and all the petticoats had embroidery as well. Jonnie had white stockings to wear and low, black shoes and a scarf to wear around her neck that would fasten below her throat with a brooch. "Are these not clothes such as dreams are made of?" Jonnie asked as she laid each piece out on her bed. "And see, white gloves. I am to be the one to carry our horn in the procession."

"Wow! Your president could not have honored you more."

She grinned and nodded. "Yes, this will be a time."

Someone knocked on the tent pole. "Hello? Jonnie?"

"Hi, Pavle. Come on in and join us." Sondra indicated a space on her bed for him to sit.

Pavle looked around. "Sorry, I can't stay. There are already some people from the press here. They will be over in a couple of minutes to meet Jonnie. I've also asked two of the older women who know our costumes to help you get ready tomorrow."

"Thank you," Jonnie answered.

Jonnie's on her own, I reflected. I'm just the current page in the book of her life. Although, with the end of summer rapidly coming, every day was becoming more and more precious. I had mentioned Jonnie's future to Pavle and Tom. Both had promised to "do something for her." But that was all either had offered. I needed to get a firmer commitment, one that would provide for her, and protect her from Leo—should he ever come after her.

Jonnie hung her costume by its hangers from the ridge pole and gave me a weak smile. "It won't be so bad. It's only for tomorrow."

"Yeah. Anything happens, I'm here," I replied sourly.

Reporters and cameramen with camcorders and huge battery packs began to arrive. They gathered around Jonnie's front porch, asking her questions and taking short shots of her showing them her new outfit and explaining how she came to find the horn and its player. I tried to stay in the background as much as possible. This was her show and, I told myself, why draw attention to our friendship?

In bed, snug and warm under my blanket and comforter, I stared across the empty space and my tent's canvas toward Jonnie's tent. I felt a knot in my stomach and a bad taste in my mouth, lonely for the first time since my stay in that Noviastad hotel. What would this summer have been like without Jonnie? My father had promised that three months abroad would change me forever. I bit my lower lip. Why were fathers always right? "Although," I whispered to myself. "I do not think this was the change he had in mind."

"Shh."

"What? Who's there?"

"Who do you think." Jonnie planted her bottom next to my shoulders. "I'm lonely; I can't sleep. May I visit a while?"

I shifted over as far as I dared. "Sure. I was just thinking about you."

"Really? What were you thinking?" Jonnie's voice had taken on a slightly impish tone.

"I…I was thinking about how much knowing you has changed my life."

161

"Knowing you has saved my life," she answered immediately. "I'm cold. Would it be all right if I got under your comforter a little?"

"Sure." I lifted my covers. I heard Jonnie's boots "thunk" on the floor one at a time, followed by the slow "flump" of her cloak settling beside them. Then she lay down beside me with her back against my chest.

"Ouch! Your toes are like ice!"

"Ice? I do not know that word yet." She began rubbing her feet against mine. I clinched my teeth and let it happen. In a moment, I felt my heart quickening as my bare chest pressed against her slip-covered back. I slowly worked my right arm around her body until the hand was nestled between her breasts. "Is this good?"

"Mm-hm." Jonnie laid her own hands on top of mine. "Now I'm warm." A long silence followed before she spoke again. "Jim, what's going to happen in two weeks when you go back to America?"

"I don't know." Then I said the words I had been thinking almost every day for the last month. "I wish you were going with me."

"In what way?"

I had to think about that a moment. How could a sixteen-year-old girl go with a nineteen-year-old college student back to America? Truth? Tell her the truth! "I would want you to go as my special girl...as the love of my life."

"Oh." That was all she said, but she pressed herself closer and, rotating my hand, placed it on her right breast. I could smell her now, her hair against my face, sweet and clean, her body slightly musky but good. Never had the presence of any female caused me so much excitement, or so much confusion and sadness. Tom's words from our first conversation concerning Jonnie kept coming back, spoiling these magic minutes. "...don't get any ideas about taking her home with you in August." How was this to end? Once I left, were we ever to see each other again? A sob trickled out.

She heard and was turning over and taking me in her still thin arms, clasping my head in her hands and drawing me to her lips. "Please, be gentle," she said.

I nodded as best I could and kissed her, aware that my mustache must be scratching her nose. Her mouth opened slightly and received me anyway. "Again?" she asked after I had paused to come up for air. "I have never done this before. Only watched the others in the spirits garden."

"Jonnie-anna, you are the most wonderful kisser in the world." Those were the only words I managed before she covered my mouth again.

Later I turned onto my back and she snuggled against me, her left hand cradling my neck and head. "I love you," I told her in English. She answered the same in Starnovian. Somehow, saying those words made any future possible.

Chapter 26

Dawn was just beginning to penetrate the tent when Jonnie sat up, slipped her boots onto her bare feet, wrapped her cloak around her shoulders and left.

I lay still, watching the first shadows from the trees high on the mound start their creep across the tent's roof. My shoulders hurt, and I had barely slept at all. I closed my eyes again, trying to comprehend the explosion of emotions I had experienced and what they meant. Too much had happened—too much that could not be undone. But I did not want a different path. Wherever this love was going to take us, I was happy to follow it.

The ceremonies were to begin at 10 o'clock, to be followed by a luncheon for the president, his cabinet and other important guests. Dr. Bayar had gotten an invitation as representative for Turkey. Tom and the American Ambassador were also going to be present, along with representatives from the United Nations and other neighboring countries. Tom promised me a seat in the tent. That was all. I felt a little resentment, but promised myself not to spoil this special day for Jonnie.

Long before breakfast was over, the trucks, motorcycles and cars began arriving, the guards directing the general public to an area near the gate cleared for use as a lot.

At 8 o'clock the two Starnovian women and Sondra gathered in Jonnie's tent to help her dress. I was almost dressed myself when I heard a commotion next door. "How's it goin', you guys?" I called.

"We're coming over," Sondra answered. "Jonnie insists that you must be the one to comb and braid her hair."

"Of course," I chuckled.

"He will not do it; he is a man," the elder of the two Starnovians, a stout woman in a red *kabusha* exclaimed as Jonnie entered my tent.

"And why wouldn't I?" I replied. Jonnie grinned, handed me her comb and sat down with her back to me. I began to pull out her braid. She already had the skirt, petticoats and stockings on and was finishing the securing of the blouse front as I worked.

I soon finished. "There. All ready. Do you have a ribbon?"

"Here." she handed me a blue one the same shade as the flowered kabusha. I tied it in a neat bow and gave her a light tap on her backside to let her know I was finished.

"Oh-ho," the Starnovian women laughed.

"He's one to watch out for," the elder woman added.

"No, he has to watch out for her," the other replied. "Already she has him waiting on her like he's her servant."

Jonnie smiled at me, our hands touched, and we exchanged a kiss.

"Oh, Holy Mother! Now I know what's been happening all these nights!" the older woman cried out in mock horror.

"Watch it, guys," Sondra added. "Keep this up, and pretty soon everyone will think you're Bob and Ilona's replacements." Still chuckling, Jonnie and her three companions headed back to the other tent.

When I saw Jonnie again, she had added a dark blue shawl of light-weight wool printed with yellow and gold lines that picked up the gold threads in her blouse. A large silver brooch held it in place around her shoulders. Against her throat she wore the silver chain she had bought for herself and over her hair she wore the flowered *kabusha*. She stood on the edge of her platform, gloved hands clasped in front, and tilted her head down shyly. "Does this look respectable for my president?"

"Is that whom you are wearing the *kabusha* for?" I asked.

"Everything I wear today is for my people—except the *kabusha*. That I wear for you." Her attendants nodded to each other. She gave me a faint smile. "Do I still look only fourteen? Or, maybe I look more sixteen, as I am?"

I smiled and nodded. Never had Jonnie looked more grown up. "You are a wonder." I said.

She lightly stepped off the platform and offered me her hand. "You look all dressed up yourself."

I shrugged. It had taken me fifteen minutes to find my only tie, and I had had to borrow Sondra's iron to get my one halfway-decent shirt in a wrinkle-free condition. I was wearing my workboots since they, at least, were leather and took a polish. All my other footgear was jogging shoes or sandals. "It's the best I have here."

"Escort me now," she said.

"You're my royal princess."

"And you are my American prince." Then we both laughed and started toward the pavilion set up next to the museum site.

"If you cannot come with me in August," I said. "You must write me by E-mail."

"Do you have an address at your home?"

"Yes, both at home and at school. I will give them to you this afternoon."

"And I will give you my home address, in case I must go back to my village and family. Maybe we will not need them, but nothing is certain yet. Yes?"

"Nothing is certain yet," I answered—although I knew my heart was sure.

The president proved to be short and gray-haired and his speech boring, if sincere. The Bishop of Noviastad, the Metropolitan of the Starnovian Orthodox church and the head of the Lutheran Synod did a joint service together, then an honor guard of soldiers all decked out in gold braid carried out a blue casket covered with the Starnovian flag. Jonnie, carrying the horn, its golden surface flashing in the sunlight, followed the casket. The soldiers set the casket down in front of a new crypt, and Jonnie handed the horn to the lead horn player of the Starnovian National Orchestra. He placed his lips over the mouthpiece and one gloved hand in the bell and began the Starnovian national anthem. The rest of the orchestra joined in on the second stanza. The crowd began to sing too, although many were having a difficult time due to crying. My own eyes brightened as I felt the horn player's pride. When the anthem ended, he placed the horn carefully on the casket, immediately on top of the horn on the flag, stepped back and saluted. Everyone else, including the president, saluted as well. The clergy gave a final blessing, and the ceremony was over.

The crowd was breaking up. Jonnie was coming toward me, radiating both happiness and relief. I waved to make sure she saw where I was standing and started toward her through the crowd. Our eyes met, hers moved past me and her expression blinked from happiness to horror.

"Jonnie?" I spun around. Leo was standing fewer than three people away, his jaw set, his eyes hard and a pistol in his hand.

I did not think, I reacted—training and instinct moving my hand to the dirk and my legs driving my body toward this man in one instant of time. I shoved a woman aside and sprang at Leo, the knife contacting his abdomen even as I hit his neck with my free hand. An explosion rang in my ear, deafening me.

Time became a sand-trickle as Leo and I embraced. He had missed and lost the gun, and I had him. "I'm sorry," I whispered. Fingers slipping and clawing at his sweaty, stubble-covered throat, I pulled him around and my eyes again met Jonnie's.

She was still standing where she had been a second earlier, hands against her brooch, but her eyes no longer saw me. A stain was slowly spreading from the area of her left upper chest, turning the white of her blouse and gloves a dark red and pulling the color from her face—leaving only the freckles on her nose. "Jonnie!" In a sudden fury, I jammed my dirk into Leo then jerked it sideways, never minding or noticing the gush of blood that move released. I let go of the dirk and pushed through the panicked crowd toward her crying "Jonnie, Jonnie," over and over, as if, by calling to her, I could block the grasp and pull of the boatman that clearly showed on her face.

Tom drove me to the airport that night. The authorities had the plane for New York via London held and waiting for me. Pavle swore that all my belongings were with me. I knew my computer, my papers, my digital assistant and my camera were in the Land Rover. I did not care about anything else. I didn't really care about anything.

Tom said nothing the entire trip, but at the gate he gripped my shoulder. "It was vendetta blood. There won't be charges. Everyone, even the president, understands. And, Jim...I'm sorry. I know you had grown close to her, but, think about it: this fall it would have been over."

Hearing those last words sparked an anger so deep I found myself wanting to spit in his hypocritical face. I could not shake his hand or even look at him. Instead, I just walked away. That was the last time I ever spoke with Dr. Brothers.

Part VII: Newark Airport

Chapter 27

The first thing I did that fall when I got back to school was change my major from archaeology to a history and geography combination. I knew I never wanted to take another course with Dr. Brothers, or have him as my advisor. The change meant I would have to take summer courses in order to graduate in four years, but I didn't care. I wrote up my summer report and turned it in through the mail. I later discovered Tom had given me an 'A'. I flipped a bird at the grade slip.

I wrote Pavle several times in September and October trying to find out exactly what had happened to Jonnie, but never received any replies. This really ticked me off. The place had gone crazy after I stabbed Leo. One guard must have thought I had been the one who shot Jonnie because while I was standing there staring at her dying, he started beating me on the head. Emil, yelling and waving his arms, stopped him, then somehow got me off the field and to his tent. "Wait here," he told me. "I will find out how Jonnie is." He never came back. I waited, hungry and half-covered with Leo's blood for four hours, desperate to go somewhere, talk to anyone, get changed—yet afraid if I did, I would miss Emil. Finally Tom showed up instead—with a clean shirt, and word that I was leaving. When I tried to ask him what had happened to Jonnie, he only shook his head.

As I settled back into life at home, I did try to put Jonnie and my own feelings of guilt and love behind me, but she kept reappearing in strange ways, some of them predictable, some not. Hundreds of pictures of her were waiting for me in my room at home. In a way, they helped. It was easier to look at Jonnie, still alive and smiling, busy at the dig, or bashfully hamming with Sondra in front of their tent, than remember my last sight of her—leaning against a medic, every breath dribbling blood down her chin, every breath a short, pain-filled, wordless agony. I finally picked out two and got them framed: a copy of the first picture I had taken of her just outside my tent, and another I had taken three days before the ceremony—one a skinny girl, one a grown-up. I set them on my desk but rarely had the courage to look at them.

Half my clothes did not make it back with me, but a pair of Jonnie's underwear and one of her books did. I had no idea how or why they ended up in my stuff. The book was a gray, tattered paperback, a romance about a prince and a girl set in a time long ago. I felt sick in my stomach seeing these things—the only items I had that she had owned. How I wished there was something else of hers—like a pin, or pressed flowers. I gently placed the underwear and book in an old shoebox and stored them in my bottom dresser drawer.

Forgetting Jonnie seemed to be the smart thing to do. I knew I wanted to go on to graduate school. Carrying a torch for a girl killed half a world away due to my own recklessness did not read like a good game plan. When I started the fall semester, I put the pictures away and when my parents and friends asked questions, refused to talk about her. That plan held for that school year.

I also resolved never to let my gut instincts guide my physical reactions again in my life. A single *demkos* with a hole drilled through it and hung by a string around my neck became my daily reminder of that promise to myself.

The next summer I took a full course load and by that fall I was sure I had worked Jonnie and my guilt out of my system. I began to hang out with girls and even date—although such encounters all seemed to end in sadness or indifference. I also began to take a renewed interest in current Starnovian affairs, stopping by the library to read the latest issues of the *Economist* and scanning the *New York Times*. In September the *Economist* ran a picture of the new museum at Castelschtop and all the memories of that summer came flooding back. I checked *Der Spiegel* and found a color picture there as well. The building looked rather severe, I thought, but the article promised that the grounds would be planted with many roses. If true, I approved. The article did not mention Jonnie at all.

The Institute had continued the dig and had found hundreds of more bodies, buried in the rubble. These included the bodies of what were believed to be King Stephen, his queen and daughter. Unlike the bodies found by the south wall, these still had their weapons and appeared to have died fighting. Why the bodies had not been stripped remained an unanswered question.

I read this and reflected that if someone asked Emil, he probably could find an answer. That in turn gave me a thought. I had been trying for weeks to think of an idea for my senior thesis. Maybe I could write an account of the Turkish-Starnovian War of 1684 using Turkish documents for a fresh viewpoint.

I had already searched the college's catalogues and run an on-line search of periodical databases when I decided to add a WEB search to my effort, just to make sure I had hit all bases. The Starnovian government had its own site with a link to a site for the museum. I stared at the highlighted words. Was I ready for this? Jonnie was over a year-and-a-half ago. I closed my eyes, remembering the dust and dry heat, the cold tent at night and...Jonnie. Talking to Jonnie in the evenings about what we had done or found, what we should concentrate on the next day, talking to Jonnie about America and about her people, talking about life. My hand grasped the mouse, but I could not press the button. Would it ever work? Would I ever forget?

I did my senior thesis on the Dutch defeat of the Spanish in their war for independence. That spring I tried a serious girlfriend, a chubby, noisy woman my age who lighted up every social occasion with laughter and happy conversations. The first weeks went well but soon, every time I smelled her fragrance, I remembered Jonnie's own distinct, earthy smell when she joined me for supper each evening—a combination of bath soap and the dust of Castelschtop. When this woman and I hugged and kissed, I remembered Jonnie's slender body against mine. When she laughed, I remembered Jonnie's tears. I ended the relationship in April before I graduated.

On the other hand, my first year of graduate studies at Penn State went well and that next summer I finally thought myself ready to tackle the Turkish-Starnovian War. Once more I dug out all the material Emil had sent me, surprised at how much there was. I went through the university's library holdings, which were more extensive than my undergraduate school's had been, and I ordered materials through interlibrary loan. By September I had a rough draft for a thesis that ran to just over two hundred pages.

My advisor's response? "Have you been in touch with this Dr. Bayar—the man who provided you with the original materials?"

I did not have the right answer to that question. Had I been avoiding contacting him? Would he unavoidedly touch on the one subject I still could not bear to deal with? "No, I haven't. But I will."

I had written Pavle. I had asked him about Jonnie. He had never answered. Tom Brothers might have known what happened to her, but I knew I would rather herd swine than contact him. Why hadn't I contacted Emil? I could not answer my own question.…I still had his old E-mail address. Was it because he had, in effect, abandoned me that afternoon in Castelschtop? I logged on, checked my E-mail and opened a new document.

Dear Dr. Bayar:

I am sorry to be just writing you now after such a long silence. I am starting my second year of graduate work at the Pennsylvania State University and have begun to plan my master's thesis. I would like to do it on the Turkish-Starnovian War of 1684. I would like to use the materials you found for us three years ago. Are you still working in this area? Have any new materials shown up? I may be reached at...

I studied the document. I had done it. Should I also ask about Jonnie? I stared at the screen—remembering—the sickness of guilt and despair already started. She had died because of my doing, because of my quick, never-thinking response. No, let it go for now. I clicked on the "send" box without adding anything.

Chapter 28

Emil replied two days later.

"This is wonderful news," he wrote. "Send me your current bibliography. I will be glad to check it and add to it. I am still working with UNESCO. We have found and added many more documents to the ones you had three years ago. I go to Mellankos and Castelschtop almost every month. In fact, I will be there next week. Would you like me to say hello to those who remember you and still ask about you?"

Who would remember me? Pavle?

The reply continued. "We have often wondered what happened to you. We asked Tom Brothers, but he did not answer. He has not worked with us since that summer. We thought maybe you did not want to have anything to do with this place. You were, after all, almost killed here. Tell us how you are. We are so glad to hear that you are still a scholar and now doing graduate work."

This was good news. Emil was the one person from that summer I still trusted. If he said he would check my list, he would do it. I replied:

> "Thank you for your generous offer of support. I will add my complete list of sources as an attachment to this E-mail. Please look it over and add, comment or change it as you see fit. Yes, I am definitely interested in any additional materials you might have, Turkish or Starnovian. Thank you. JIM GAILEY."

Should I add anything about myself? How I was now? I paused, then typed. "I am well, still grieving for Jonnie and missing her, but getting on with my work." Should I say that? Did it sound unprofessional, even sappy? I stared at the screen, my anger rising. So what! I loved that girl. Why shouldn't I say I missed her? I hit the "send" box.

When I checked my E-mail the next morning, a message from a "jaguar@cast.antiq.star" was waiting for me. I did not recognize the address. The letter read:

Dear Jim,

Emil sent me your E-mail address. I hope it is okay that I write you. Emil said that you are well. Please, tell me what has happened to you. It would be all right if you do not want to, but I have wondered. I think of you often.

Sincerely,
Jonneanna Gilenhoff
Castelschtop Site Assistant

Neighbors living in my apartment building told me later that they clearly heard my screams of joy that morning two floors away.

Dear Jonnie,

I thought you were dead. No one ever told me you were alive. No one ever wrote me. If this is a dream, please, let it be true!!! How quickly can I see you?

I Love you, JIM.

Jonnie: Emil paid for the ticket. I was on a flight to Newark via Frankfurt four days later. All those days, Jim and I wrote and wrote and even spoke by phone, typing and talking desperately as we tried to catch up with those missing three years. I had to tell him that my only memory of the shooting was seeing him covered with blood and knowing he was dead. I did not remember anything else, not even my own wound, which just missed my heart but passed through my left lung, leaving me sick and weak for such a long time that I could not write or even get out of bed. I also explained how—once I knew Jim was alive—I had written Dr. Brothers several times, but had never gotten a reply. I told him how our president had personally seen to it that, after I recovered, I had a job at Castelschtop where I had become the chief writer and recorder of artifacts.

Poor Pavle shook his head often during those four days. "I am losing you forever, I know that," he told me many times, but he got me the visa papers and made sure I had a ride to the airport when the time came.

Jim later told me that he was on the Interstate highway out of State College by five o'clock that morning. The plane was late taking off from Frankfurt, and we had strong headwinds. I got sick twice. When we finally landed, the American customs officials insisted on opening and looking through all my luggage.

Jim: By eleven I was in the concourse waiting, a dozen red roses in hand. I waited over an hour, alternately hopeful and frustrated. I was sure I would know her when I saw her, but the tall, slender, tired-looking woman wearing glasses—carrying a rucksack and pushing a cart with two suitcases and accordion case in it—was not quite what I envisioned. She came out slowly, hesitating, scanning the waiting crowd. Then I knew, the long dark hair in a single braid down her back the giveaway. "Jonnie?" I called.

She saw me, and the fatigue and years fell away. "Oh, Jonnie!" I walked—almost running, really—toward her, but before I could reach her, she reached into her rucksack and took out the *Kabusha* of our dreams and tied it on her head.

Then we hugged and kissed and, this time, both of us cried without shame or hesitation.

The End

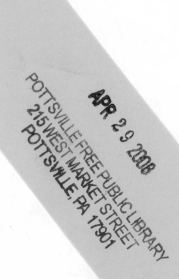
Printed in the United States
108972LV00001B/64/A

9 781424 189274